The DEADLY MAILMAN

FROM THE AUTHOR OF THE U.S. MARSHAL HARRY BAILEY
Parables of Life Series

The CASE of

I0538239

THE

DEADLY

MAILMAN

Author Minister Larry Montgomery, Sr.

montgomerybusiness@hotmail.com

The DEADLY MAILMAN

ISBN: 978-0-9861290-2-5

Published by Emerging Business Group, Inc.

Baldwin, New York.

The DEADLY MAILMAN

Dedicated to my wife Joyous and my children
for their love and support.

The DEADLY MAILMAN

ABOUT THE AUTHOR

Minister Larry Montgomery, Sr., is a retired Banker currently publishing the only weekly online African-American community newspaper on Long Island. Minister Montgomery, Sr. holds a MBA from Hofstra University, Hempstead, New York where he grew up, married and raised three loving children.

As a member of Glory Temple Ministries, Inc., under the Pastorship of Senior Pastor Apostle Ronnie Deadwyler and Executive Pastor Apostle Dr. Karen Deadwyler, who in obedience to the Father, planted the seed of "Scribe" on Minister Montgomery's heart: To that end, Minister Montgomery committed to penning twelve (12) of the Lord's parables under the cover of the life and times of a fictional character named U.S. Marshal Harry Bailey. Look for "A Special Anniversary Edition of "U.S. Marshal Harry Bailey the case of the Corporate Killings" and all of our other works on our web-site at www.usmarshalharrybailey.com.

Those two projects are now complete. Since then he has written six other new fictional short stories entitled; "The Game of Your Life", "The Way Station", Beyond 'The Way Station' Part II—To Hell for the Holidays, "Clinical Trial's", "2-1-1 Emergency" Dial in case of murder, "Criminal Mastermind". Upcoming projects scheduled for release in 2013-2014 include: "The Day After Life"-The Way Station The Final Chapter, "Real Families in the Ghetto--40 years in NYCHA (Part 1), "Dilemma" and "The APP" Click Here for Murder.

We hope you find a few moments of reading pleasure from each of these projects. And we ask that you look forward to our 2014-2015 U.S. Marshal Harry Bailey projects a six volume series entitled: "U.S. Marshal Harry Bailey and the City of Prophesy" you won't be disappointed.

May God continue to Bless You and Yours!

The DEADLY MAILMAN

ABOUT THIS BOOK:

John Mason is playing the game of multi-million dollar monopoly and he is only six key properties away from winning. It has taken him 18 years of wheeling and dealing to get to this point and the only thing that could stop him was time, something he was quickly running out of time. A special election to fill an untimely City Council seat vacancy was just announced. And John realized that his parking garage empire maybe doomed to fail before it even got started. City Councilman Mark Oliver's seat was just abruptly vacated and a special election to replace him has been set for this coming September 30th less then 6 months away. John knows that without Mark Oliver on the City Council all chances for the development of a new sports stadium will die and so would possibilities for his parking lot empire along with the almost $40 million dollars in increase real estate values for properties he had already purchased. All of John's hard work and time spent picking up properties surrounding the site for the new stadium would have been for not. Years ago John set out to become one of the most powerful real estate developers in the City and this project was going to be the crown jewel in his empire. John Mason the Private Parking Lot King of New York City is now desperate.

But this crown will only be a fawn memory if John doesn't secure the purchase rights to the last six properties before the special election. Follow John's master plan to secure those last six properties by making the owners a final take it or leave it offer via special delivery mail.

The problem is each of the six property owners keep turning up dead and no one knows why. This is one of Marshal Harry Bailey's most baffling cases and just when he catches on to the why and the who, the mastermind winds up dead.

Sit back and follow this investigative nightmare entitled the case of the Deadly Mailman and see if you can figure out what kind of parcels John Mason is really having delivered.

The DEADLY MAILMAN

TABLE OF CONTENTS

See page for a list of other U.S. Marshal Harry Bailey's cases page 234

INTRODUCTION

6:00 am Monday, April 9th 1983—Mahwah Prison, New Jersey Cell 3105

There was a loud knock on the cell gate and the guard yelled out, "On the Gate...3105, New Fish." Then the cell door opened and in walked Roscoe Jenkins. The toilet was stopped up and the sink hadn't worked in three days so his cell make Lou Gallo was quiet rip. As the guard closed the cell door behind Roscoe he knocked on the gate again and yelled, "On the gate ... 3105, Lock it up." As he walked away he turned and looked back into the cell at the still standing Roscoe and the sleeping Lou Gallo and said, "Now you two play nice."

Roscoe took a look around and started to gag from the smell then he kicked the bottom bunk where Lou was laying with his back to the wall and the blanket over his head and said, "Wake up. Wake Up. You're in my bed."

Lou didn't move. Roscoe became more aggressive and kicked the bunk three more times, each harder than the last and continued to yell, wake up you're in my bed. Finally Roscoe reached over with his right hand and grabbed the blanket over Lou's head and snatched it back. With that his right arm was extended back and away from his body and that was when Lou rose and stuck a six inch shive up under Roscoe's arm pit and grabbed him around his Addams-apple and said, "Welcome to my Hell. Your bunk is on the floor in the corner next to the toilet, any questions?"

Not knowing whether to crap or go blind Roscoe settled himself and said, "Man you crazy" and slowly backed away dropping the blanket. Lou eased up out off of the bunk bed and pressed the shive harder into Roscoe's arm pit and said, "That blanket you just dropped...is mine. Pick it up and place it back on the bed or this will be the shortest sentence you ever served." Roscoe meekly complied and after he put the blanket back on the bunk he raised his hands in the air and said, "Look man no need in getting up set and doing anything rash. I was just trying to get your attention. No harm, no foul, ok? Sorry. Can we start over?"

Lou pulled back the shive and sat back on his bunk and said, "Sure, why not; now that you have interrupted my beauty sleep. What's your name and what are you in for?"

Roscoe sat on the floor right between the toilet and the cell door and said, "My name is Roscoe, Roscoe Jenkins. I'm from Brooklyn, the Red Hook section but they picked me up in Newark on some bull. A dupe charge and I wasn't even involved. I was just a victim of circumstance, you know. They gave me 7 to 10 but I should be out in 42 months. Whats your name and your tail of woe?"

Lou said, "My name is Lou but you can call me Pop's. I'm in under false pretenses as well. They pinned a murder on me. So I got life but right now it's under appeal. That's why I'm still in the general population. I been waiting five years but my lawyer tells me that it will all work out. You know?"

Both men looked at each other and smiled and then busted out laughing.

Roscoe said, "I like you, Pop's. How old are you, man?"

Lou said, "I tell everyone I'm 42 but they tell me I look like I'm 32 can you believe that?" Roscoe said, "Turn around and let me see your face from the back maybe I'll believe them." Both men busted out laughing again.

Lou smiled and said, "You want to die up in this place?" Roscoe said, "Hell no. I got a baby girl and one on the way. I just want to do my time and get right." Lou said, "You got a girl outside?" Roscoe said, "I was about to get married until I screwed up. Now I don't just don't know. She said, she would wait but man 42 months is a long time, you feel me?"

Lou said, "I been here 63 months, I feel you. But I'm good. Got a few things going, on the outside. I'm gonna be alright whenever I get out. Planning, that's what it's all about; planning."

Roscoe said, "I hear you man, I hear you. So tell me about you pop's. Where did it all go wrong, man?"

Lou said, "What are you a cop? Why you all up in my business?"

8:00 pm Tuesday, May 13th 1983—Mahwah Prison, New Jersey Cell 3105

Lou finally spoke to Roscoe again and said, "I want to tell you a story about a guy I used to know, you interested?" Roscoe looked at him in complete surprise and said, "You talking to me?" Lou said, "Ain't nobody else in here for me to talk to, is there? Of course I'm talking to you. You want to hear the story or what?"

Roscoe shook his head yes and said, "Man you haven't spoken a word to me in what six weeks. Not even a damn hello and now you ask me if I want to hear a story about some guy you used to know. Ya I want to hear something other than your snoring, go ahead, tell me something."

Lou sat back on his bunk and said, "I used to sell life insurance but before that I was a wish guy, up and coming. I had a knack for acting so sometimes I would shake people down for the bosses by pretending to be an undercover cop or a Fed looking into a case. It was a lot of fun but then it became serious or maybe it just became serious to me. I just got off on it the rush. I couldn't help myself. I pushed these roles to the limit and it just gave me a high I couldn't explain. You know playing a role or pretending to be somebody and not knowing when of it the person I was talking to was ever going to figure it out."

Lou continued and said, "So one day I was told to pick up a bet from this insurance broker, Sam Gold. Now Old Man Gold was a nice guy. He lived alone and he did pretty good but he liked to gamble and he was awful at it. This time when the bosses sent me over to collect, Sam had gotten way behind. The bosses told me I should make am example of this guy, eventhough he was a long time good customer. Didn't mean anything to me but I wondered why kill the goose that laid the golden egg? Especially since he was still able to lay eggs!

So when I got to his house he knew why I was there and he came clean, he said he was waiting for some money from one of his policyholders and he would make good as always. I tried to explain that that wasn't enough. The boss was very unhappy and somebody had to go. It just was his day to go. So when I put the .22 to his head he pleaded, cried, pleaded, I mean this guy cried so much so fast I got confused. Then he said, he had an idea. I'm thinking these are this old guy's last words, so what the heck. Let me at least listen before I whack him.

Now listen to this, he told me if I would just let him leave he would walk away and never come back, and I could have everything he had, just don't kill him. That got my attention, so I said to him what's in it for me? You can't even pay your gambling debt. He said, but I got money coming, as soon as one of my policyholders dies I'm gonna get paid. I said, what you think I'm an idiot the policyholders beneficiary gets paid what you gonna get? He said, he always puts his name on the policy as the beneficiary for a piece of the action just incase the policy lapses. He can keep it going for a short time until the policyholder gets on his feet again. He had a lot of old customer's; anyone of them was ready to kick the bucket any day now.

So I thought about it, and I thought about it, and I thought about. I said tell me what he thought I should do. He said, look just pretend that I was his son and was helping out in the business while I was sick. I said, what about a license. You need a license to do this, don't you? He said, just use mine. Be me.

So I asked him where would he go and what would he do? He said, he would go away and do what he always did, gamble and work hard. So I shot him.

That's what I do. I buried him in the back yard and then I brought his right hand to the bosses and they paid me.

Then I went back to the old guy's house and started pretending to be him. I figured I would contact his clients tell them I was helping my uncle out for a few months while he was in cancer care or something and they could continue to send their checks in to me. In my name you know. I stopped paying the premiums for a while until I realized that when they died they would need to get their money or their beneficiary would want the money so came up with this plan.

I would select the oldest, sickest, loneliness, go put them out of their misery and cash the benefits check, catch up on all of the past due policy payments and then go do it again for the gravy.

Got so good I actually started selling insurance to the beneficiaries of the old guys clients over the phone most of them I didn't even have to go see. I learned a lot about selling insurance too.

After a while I would go and write phony policies on people I'd already killed or figured would be dead within the year because I had planned to kill them. I laid my policies off to three different small reinsurance companies so there wasn't a lot of follow up or questions, they were just happy to get the business.

Sometimes I would have to go and kill the policyholder and hide the body for a few months before making the claim; just to keep my claim turnover in line with what the insurance company thought made since. I guess they don't want all of your policyholders to die on the same day, you know. Thank God I found out that Old man Gold had a small pig farm upstate where I could dispose of the bodies from time to time. I learned about that by watching the discovery channel, you know."

Just then the jail loud speaker went off and the pod guard told everyone out of their cells, it was a surprise inspection so the two men had to leave the cell and wait outside while the cell was searched.

Once the search was over they returned and Lou picked up were he left off.

Lou started to speak again and said, "Yea, things were going great. I had just become next in line to be a made man, I had plenty of money in my pocket and my impersonation scam was going great. See one of the benefits of becoming a made man is you get your own operation, you wear better fitting suits and drive great cars. I had a great car and wore fine suits so all I had to look forward to was what kind of an operation the bosses would chose for me. This is not something that you go in and negotiate for; you gladly take what they give and do the best job you can with it, or else.

Since I really didn't tell anybody about my insurance scam I was able to keep the proceeds to myself, man was that a lot of work. But anyway, the bosses got around to offering me a freelance franchise. You know murder for hire. They would send me out or hire me out to do jobs that require a certain amount of expertise. They knew I could do something's on my own but they felt why not keep a rope around my neck and their hand in my pocket, and my insurance scam gave me the greatest flexibility.

Now with my franchise I was asked what my M.O. would be. I said, I would be the mail man. You know the guy who delivers. That cracked them up. Next thing I knew I was getting good business. You know when I was an underling I could get $5 maybe $10 large for a hit. When I got my franchise I was making $25 to $50 large. I mean the hits were more substantial though. I was always concerned with getting caught and losing my franchise. So I had to keep on my toes, you know.

The bosses would send me to meet the mark

sometimes, sometimes they would tell me how they wanted him killed, and it was hard work. Sometimes these guys would be so mad at a person they would just want them dead. Where ever they were when I saw them, they wanted them dead, right there and then. But most of the time I was able to convince them that a certain amount of poetic justice could bring them additional satisfaction and keep me out of jail. So it got to the point that they would just give me the name and let me do what I do best, you know.

Now things were going great until the bosses made me an offer I couldn't refuse. I mean that literally too. They knew that I knew if I would have said no to this last job that they were going to have to have me whacked and replaced so I had no choice but to take it. This John Mason character was a piece of work too. I was told by the bosses that I was to befriend this guy Mason, stay close to him and if and when I found out what was really going on with him I was to whack him right then and there and then tell them.

Now I didn't know what or who this guy was but I quickly found out. I mean the benefit for this type of job is if you do a good job you can write your own ticket and the down side is if you

The DEADLY MAILMAN

don't do a good job you could wind up in here. So go figure. Now let me tell you about John Mason..."

CHAPTER 1

JOHN MASON
PARKING LOT KING

John Mason is a 39 year old, clean shaved, bald head, muscular looking short white man with big bug-eyed. He say's he suffers from a vitamin deficiency but most people just think he is butt ugly. John is the high school graduate who failed shop class but made it big. He is the majority partner in the largest parking lot operating company in the City of New York and he wears that like a badge of honor.

John plays hard, drinks hard, loves harder and leaves a wake of scorched bodies everywhere he goes when it comes to picking up properties that do best as parking lots. From a 60' x 120' lot in the Bronx to a six story underground lease operation in lower Manhattan John and his partner Fred Beckett are considered the kings of parking in the City of New York.

John's best and only friend Fred Beckett have been together for over 15 years making money hand over fist in the parking lot management business. Fred a retired widowed real estate lawyer takes care of the back office while John focuses on selection and set up. Fred is about 60 years old but he looks amazingly young for his age. Many people still think he is around 40 years old. Fred has three grown children, none of whom are in the business of law or parking lots and six school aged grandchildren. His wife died several years ago in an auto accident. Fred hasn't been the same since.

Both Fred and John live on Long Island on the north shore in the Great Neck area, another deal orchestrated by Fred. The men bought one lot and built two homes on it right on the bay.

The keys to John and Fred's success belong to Fred's wife's inheritance and a City Councilman named Mark Oliver a former law partner of Fred's. Mark Oliver a graduate of City College and NYU Law thinks of himself as the one that got robbed of the love of his life, Fred's deceased wife Mary Jane. The three go back to high school in the Long Beach area. When Mary Jane opted to marry Fred, Mark could not just walk away so he did everything he could to stay close to her even taking Fred on as a full partner in his father's law firm. In their later years after Fred proved himself and Mark won his first term on the City Council, Mark was compelled to help Fred pick up as many vacant city lots as he could for development. It wasn't until John Mason came along that they realized they had a gold mine in parking lot space then in residential or commercial structures.

A typical small parking lot can earn as much as a $100,000 a year after expenses if properly managed; and when John meet Lou Gallo the Mason Beckett parking lot empire was bringing in over $30 million dollars a year before expenses and taxes.

About five years before John Mason meet Lou Gallo, John and Fred had embarked on a property acquisition drive to acquire as many prospective properties as possible, without raising any suspicions in the downtown Brooklyn area. At first they wanted to buy up or lease, or control properties along Flatbush and Atlantic Avenue's. Rumors had, had it that a new sports arena was about to be built there and parking would be at a premium. So John and Fred went about slowly and methodically acquiring properties at discounted prices. As the time of final approval for the development got closer the price of land, improved or not started going through the roof and even higher once landlords got wind of multiple purchases of adjacent lots. John and Fred were able to gather many parcels earlier on because of inside information from Councilman Oliver. But there did come a point when the project was finally approved and the cat was out of the bag many property owners were looking to cash in on the development prospects.

Lou Gallo Meets John Mason at the Law Offices of Oliver, Beckett and Oliver

As John Mason sat in the lobby of the law offices of Oliver, Beckett and Oliver waiting to speak to Councilman Oliver in walked Lou Gallo who was returning from the restroom. Lou walked over and sat in the chair across from John. As Lou sat he spoke and said, "Hello" and picked up a magazine and started to read it. John looked up and somewhat stun responded and said, "What happened? I thought you were on bed rest." Lou looked up kind of confused and looked around and then said, "Are you talking to me, buddy?"

John smiled and said, "What is this some kind of a joke, what the hell is going on here Fred? Buddy, since when are we buddies?"

Lou looking more perplexed responded and

said, "Look my friend I think you got me mixed up with someone else, here. So let's leave it at that. Ok?"

John sat back and said, "So you really think you can pull this off?"

Lou ignored him and returned to reading his magazine. After a moment or two John stood up and reached and knocked the magazine out of Lou's hand and said, "Don't play with me like this Fred. This ain't funny. What are you doing here. You should be in the hospital, in bed, resting. Have you lost your mind or something?"

That was when the secretary came out and said, "Mr. Beckett or I'm sorry Mr. Gallo, Mr. Oliver sends his regrets but he will not be able to see you today but his son Jason is available. And Mr. Oliver wanted me to tell you that Jason is the firms senior criminal defense attorney. He would have been called into handle your case anyway. So can I direct you to his office?" Lou stood up and said, "I was told to see the old man. If he's is not available or not qualified to handle my case then I might as well go speak to my old attorney. I was trying to trade up but maybe another time. Tell him thanks anyway." Then he turned to walk out.

John stood up then and said, to the secretary, "That isn't Fred Beckett?" And she said, "Oh! No Mr. Beckett is on bed rest at Sloane Kettering I thought you knew that." John said, "Oh! Sir, sir?" as he walked behind Lou towards the elevator.

Lou continued towards the elevator and ignored him but as the elevator doors opened and he stepped in, John pushed his way inside as well. When the doors closed John reached to grab Lou's shoulder and Lou turned around so fast that his suit jacket opened and the snub-nosed .38 that he carried in his waist band was exposed. John recoiled and backed up to the door and said, "Wow, sorry sir. I just wanted to apologize for not realizing that you weren't who I thought you were. No harm no foul right?"

Lou closed his jacket and straightened his tie and didn't say anything.

As the elevator descended the two men stood quietly just looking at the floor. When the elevator finally stopped on the main floor John said, "Look I got I question and you can say yes or no and that will be it. ...Do you want to make $20,000.00?" Lou cocked his head to the right and looked at him and said, "I got $20,000.00 out in the car make it $25,000.00 and I'm listening."

John smiled and said, "$25,000.00 sounds like a negotiation meet me for dinner at the Cattlemen's Club downtown at 7:00 sharp, we'll talk, I'll bring a deposit and we'll go from there." Lou said, "Name." John said, "Oh! Yea, sorry I'm John Mason you may have heard of me? The Parking Lot King!" and he extended his hand. Lou looked at his hand and turned and walked away. When he had made about four or five steps he said, "No, never heard of ya, see you at 7:00pm sharp."

Sloan Kettering Memorial Hospital-Fred Beckett's suite

John Mason is seated at the bedside of Fred Beckett watching him sleep when Fred's son Jason Beckett walked in. Jason spoke and said, "Oh! Hello Uncle John how are you?" John smiled and stood up and hugged Jason tightly and said, "I'm fine Jason and how is everyone at home?" Jason smiled and said, "We are all fine, we were getting concerned, since we hadn't seen you much over these last few months. How is the Barclay Arena project coming along? Dad said you were getting close to securing all of the properties necessary to lock up the area's private parking business."

John sat back down and grabbed the sleeping Fred Beckett's hand and said, "We are so close but time is running out; and now this!" Jason said, "Oh! I'm glad you stopped by; the doctors have been telling us a lot of this depression maybe the result of a broken heart. He still hasn't come to grips with the death of my mother, you know." John signed and said, "He loved that lady very much and we both know he misses her a lot but I didn't think that things would start down hill so fast. I always thought he was holding up so well eventhough it always seemed he wasn't fully over it."

Jason walked over and placed his hand on John's shoulder and said, "Uncle John I was hoping once Dad gets back to work that you would talk to him about retiring again. The doctors seem to think he needs a nice long rest and this Barclay's Arena deal may not be the kind of projects that is going to help his recovery.' John looked up at Jason and said, "This Barclay's project is our ticket to freedom. This is what we have been looking for all of our lives, Jason. Your father would run me out of town if I even hinted that he should sit on the sidelines now. This is like the super-bowl of development projects. We have the chance to develop over 6,000 parking spaces in and around the municipal parking field that was designed to provide no more than half of the expected parking needs on average capacity type events. Let's not even talk about the major events like championship games, special events like concerts and the gun show. At $10 an hour or part thereof we expect to make a quarter of a million dollars per day during these events and more. Now that's real permanent dollars you hear me?"

Jason smiled and said, "So what good is a quarter, a half or even a million dollars a day or even weekend when your laid up in the hospital like he is and can't enjoy it?"

John stood up and let Fred's hand go and said, "Jason, Jason you just don't know. This is your fathers dream. This is our dream. We have an obligation to see this project through. I understand what and why you are asking me to talk to your father about retiring but I tell you this isn't going to make him feel better, this is the kind of thing that might just tear him apart."

Back in Cell Block T.W. Cell 31-05

The DEADLY MAILMAN

Lou continued to tell Roscoe about meeting John Mason a second time at the Cattlemen's Club and plotting his first major insurance policy sale.

Dinner at the Cattlemen's Club

John Mason walked into the restaurant at 6:45pm and was ushered over to his usual table in the back in the corner. As the hostess escorted him to his table he noticed that Lou was already there. Sitting and sipping on a glass of beer. John walked up, sat down and extended his hand and Lou said, "Did you bring the money?" John smiled and responded and said, "Will you take a check?" Lou smiled and said, "Only if its good." The two men smiled a devilish smile and John turned to the hostess and asked her to have the waiter bring him his usual and she left.

John looked at Lou and said, "You are an interesting fellow please tell me a little about you and what you do."

Lou smiled and said, "I thought you would never ask, but I'm in insurance one a number of levels. I sell and collect on policies from time to time. As a hobby I solve people's problems for a fee." John smiled and said, "For a fee?"

Lou smiled and said, "For a fee. Are you interested in buying some insurance?"

John smiled and said, "It depends on the policy. How do I know you can deliver the type of policy I need?"

Lou responded and said, "Once you make a purchase then the other services can come into play." John smiled and said, "What about a priority policy? How would that work?" Lou said, "First the insurance policy then the other services can come into play. Why don't I stop by your office in the morning, bring over the forms for a nice keyman insurance policy in the amount of say $1 million dollars. Will you need one for your partner as well?"

John smiled and said, "My partner may not qualify he is an older gentleman and in bad health. And at this point I'm hoping you'll be about to alleviate that problem in the very near future."

Lou smiled and said, "Why don't you tell me what you have in mind." John said, "Since you are a dead ringer for my business partner what I want you to do is impersonate him at a couple of meetings and then help him into the next life."

Lou said, "Help him into the next life? You mean kill him?"

John attempted to be hush, hush about that specific statement but he gave in and said, "Yes, exactly but it has to be done a certain way. I have it all planned out."

Lou said, "Now wait a minute, I sell insurance. I am a licensed purveyor of high quality insurance and retirement products from reputable sources. I don't kill people for a living." Then he stood up finished his drink and started to walk out. After a few steps he turned and said, "I'll see you in the morning and we will discuss your insurance needs in more detail afterwards I might reconsider your last request. Might that is." Then he walked away.

As the pod guard conducted his head count Lou continued telling his story of how he meet John Mason the NYC Parking Lot King.

The next morning around 10:00am John Mason Office

Lou stepped off of the elevator at the Hanover Square building in downtown Manhattan the 35th floor and walked into the office suite of Empire Parking Corp. where John Mason's office was.

T&e DEADLY MAILMAN

The secretary immediately ushered him into John's rather lavish office space over looking the East River. Lou looked around and found a seat while John quietly spoke on the phone. When John finally hung up Lou could tell he had just gotten some disturbing news because his whole demeanor had drastically changed since the night before, so he asked him what was wrong.

John said, "Well I need to know if you are the guy for me or not. I have run out of time and patience. So are you up for hire or not?"

Lou sat back and said, "I'm interested for the right price that is. What do you need?"

John said, "We are in the middle of a major expansion and a key resource of mine has just announced he will no longer be able to help us tie up the several key parcels to make the project work."

Lou said, "Oh! So how do I figure in?"

John said, "There are six properties out there that I need the owners to sale to me. Now we have approached all of them in the past and none of them have seen the light. I need them out of the way and I need the price to be exactly what I originally offered them. Can you make it happen?"

Lou I can make anything happen for the right price. Now what do you have in mind?"

John said, "This is what I can do, the rate is $50 large per signed contract of sale between now and September 30th. It is an all or nothing deal. And to sweeten the offer whatever you save me on each deal I'll let you keep and if you pull off all six transactions there will be a $25G bonus. Does that work for you?"

Lou thought for a moment and then he responded and said, "In addition to the $25 large you first spoke of, It will be $100 large per transaction, payable the day after each contract is laid on your desk and a $1 million bonus when it's complete." John said, "I don't have that kind of money." Lou said, "Sure you do or more precisely, sure you will. Because today I'm gonna sign you up for a $5 million dollar partnership and keyman life insurance policy that will be in full effect by the end of September. Just in time for you to pay me what you'll owe me; in full."

John said, "I already have a keyman and partnership insurance policy in that amount with a major insurance provider." Lou said, "I know,

The DEADLY MAILMAN

New York General. I also know your agents name as well. An old timer with a big book. You are gonna sign with me today if you want the full service." Then he laid a partially complete insurance policy application on John's desk with a pen.

John said, "Even if I were to go along with this, you still need to have my partner sign and I assure you not only won't he sign, but apart of your full service is gonna include taking him off of the land of the living list a.s.a.p."

Lou said, "Trust me, I already considered that before dinner last night. You just sign here and left me work out the details. Alright? Now I'm gonna need that $25 large retainer to get this ball rolling. And tell me what you had in mind for your partners going away job."

John grabbed the pen and started to sign the stack of documents, then he said, "I need you to pretend to be my partner for a few days. He's going to be coming home on bed rest tomorrow. My plan is to sneak you into his house before he arrives home, as soon as the doctor gives him a sedative, and he is under I'll have you come upstairs and we'll take him downstairs to the wine cellar hook him up to a vial of propofol and you replace him in his bedroom and just rest and relax for the next five days. Oh! Yea! You'll have to pretend as if you are losing your mind, dementia or something. I want the family to panic and think he is loosing his mind so they call in the lawyers and accountant. When they come in to start protecting the estate you'll just sign those things I need control of over to me. In the meantime I'll keep my partner on ice in the wine cellar and when it is all over you'll just get rid of him."

Lou said, Pick up the forms and took a long look at them and as he folded them up and placed them in his coat pocket he said, "Oh! No. That's not going to happen that way. When it is all over you'll get rid of him; $25 large is only enough to cover the role play. That one is gonna be on you. We don't don't want any mishaps later on. You know you thinking that since your partner looks so much like me, and he is dead, just kill me and no one will know the difference."

John said, "So what am I hiring you for?" Lou said, "To fool your partners family into thinking that your partner has lost him mind but was lucid enough to sign over those things that meant everything to you. And the securing the six other properties you need to complete your so-called parking lot empire in Brooklyn. That's what you're paying me for."

Then Lou said, "So tell me what went wrong with your contact?"

John stood up and walked over to the 15 foot windows over looking the East River and peered out and said, "Councilman Mark Oliver is being retired and a special election is going to be held in September to replace him. When that happens our lock on picking up properties in Brooklyn and having them processed without delay will be gone and it will be a free-for-all for land and commercial space sales in and around the new arena development site. So we have to finish securing those last six parcels before then."

Lou walked over to the window and stepped right into John's face and said, "So where is the retainer?" John said, "You got the retainer right there in your pocket. That life insurance policy." Lou said, "That ain't how this works my friend the insurance policy is to assure you that you'll be able to pay me when this service is over and complete the retainer is to get this service headed towards completion. And don't lose sight of the ongoing payments either. Don't get this twisted, I'm the mailman, the man who delivers and I don't work for free. And never forget no one gets rich without paying the mailman, first."

John smiled and said, "And don't you forget, no one pushes John Mason around, wait here I'll get your money." John goes over to the office wall safe and began to enter the combination. Then he said, "You study up on your acting role for tomorrow morning, be familiar with acting as if you got memory lost it help keep them from getting suspicious. Do a lot of sleeping and staring at the ceiling. Meet me here at 8:00am, I'll give you directions to the house when you get there just wait down the street far enough away that you can see who comes and goes but you can't be seen. I'll call your cellphone as I drive up. You can walk up to my car and wait in the seat behind the driver's seat. I'll park the car so that no one can see you get in or out from the house. I'll text you when you can come in the side door to the house. The door to the basement is on the left of the side door as you enter. You can go down to the wine cellar and wait there until everyone leaves. I'll keep the maid busy and until it is really clear, then I'll send her to the drug store to get his medication and we can make the switch. There is a butler's bedroom downstairs that isn't used so we can stash the old man there

The DEADLY MAILMAN

for a few hours or even days. I'll bring the sedative. Now remember you have memory lost so play that up big. We can talk a little more in the morning."

John opens the safe and counts out $25 large and hands it to Lou. Lou counts it and put it in his pocket, and said, "See you in the morning. And oh! Yea! It's a pleasure doing business with you." Then he leaves.

CHAPTER 2

SO WHAT ABOUT FRED?

Breakfast

Lou continues to tell Roscoe his story after things calm down in the mess hall

Lou continued and said, "As soon as I got back to my office I completed the policy application for John and sent it in for processing, but first I changed the beneficiary from his wife to myself. Just in case this guy tried to stiff me later on and I had to get rid of him and his body. You know some kind of fatal accident where the body is all mangled and twisted almost beyond recognition is best."

Roscoe interrupted and said, "Lou how could you make yourself the beneficiary? Aren't there laws against that?"

Lou smiled and said, "Certainly there are laws against that kind of a thing, what do you think the government is stupid or something? I used my real name. Said I was a wealthy cousin solely dependent on the income and care he provided. You think I'm stupid. I know this game."

Lou continued and said, "Now where was I? Oh! Yea, getting myself ready to play the role of a dying man who is loosing his mind, I mean memory. So the next morning I was there on time as planned and I parked down the street and watched, and watched and watched. I was there at 8:00am this fool didn't show up until 2:00pm. Talk about pissed off and I had to go to use the toilet. Good thing I brought a couple of sandwiches or I would have been nothing but skin and bones sitting there waiting for these guys."

Lou continued and said, "Well once I got into the house and took care of the immediate business things seemed to go well until that evening. I mean I got in, used the downstairs toilet while John waited out the family members who seemed like they went on forever. I mean there must have been fifty of them if there was one. I could see them pulling up in the driveway from the basement. At one time it was like a parking lot at a Knicks game there were so many cars there. Around dinner time the herd thinned out and John sent the maid out to pick up something or other and we doped up the old guy and drug him downstairs and chained him to the bed and locked the door.

That was when it got interesting. I mean I've done some acting in my day but there was no scripting this one. I took a couple of sleeping pills to avoid talking at first but by the next morning the son and daughter were all over me like a sick cat or something. I mean I could fart with someone asking if they could wipe me for God sake.

John stayed as long as he could but there came a point when even he had to go before they became too suspicious. That was when I thought it was all over. Around 2:00pm the second day, the son came in and I was woke, I had to eat you know. So he was asking me about John and this big Brooklyn arena deal. It seems that these guys never really trusted John but it was a good thing the kid liked to talk. Even when I was acting like I was asleep he would keep on talking. He told me the whole story pretty much. So finally about 5:00 o'clock or so this kid asked me I mean his father when he was going to sign the papers to buy John out or have him arrested for embezzling. I almost crapped my pants when I heard that. I mean you just can't trust anybody now-a-days.

This guy Fred had already made a case against my employer and was ready to file it when he thought taking a short rest would help prepare him for the success the two of them had worked so hard to achieve. What a partner?

This kid kept asking me to give him the ok so that was when I laid the memory lost game on him. I mean I played that so well this kid thought I was about to forget everything he had just told me before he could get his lawyer in to prepare the health proxy papers. Finally John came back the next day and the kid, the son, was in a panic he was calling his attorney, the doctor, the nurse, his mother anybody to help with the proxy papers.

I heard the doctor talking to him outside the bedroom before John stopped by with the accountant and the lawyer.

The doctor was telling him about the seven stages of dementia that he hadn't noticed anything when Fred was in the hospital but that there was no set time frame for the disease to progress. He said, basically you could be hear one moment with occasional memory lost and the next you can't remember that you needed to go to the toilet or how to feed yourself, or when to feed yourself for that matter.

So the lawyer came in alone at first and he just wanted to know if I was of sound mind, you know, if I recognized him or not. He fired a couple of true false questions then he told me what John wanted to do. I could see that he was against it but he knew his opinion really didn't count for much in certain areas. I figured as long as the family was well taken care of he wasn't going to ask to many questions. But you see he was already privy to the case Fred had built against John so I had to be cautious. I played him for a while and then I just said, look if I give him what he wants he can go away and leave us alone. I'll sell him full ownership and give him some good terms that should make everyone happy. The lawyer, now he was no dummy, he asked me how could I trust John to pay the debt off. I said, it really didn't matter to me, because I was going to sell the debt to someone else and let them worry about collecting or being his partner.

He asked me who would be trusting enough to trust John after what he did to you over all of these years. I said, I had some people in mind and he said he needed to know who before he would prepare the papers. He said they one had to be able to pay me and two had to be in a position to manage John and the business in his eyes. I gave him the number to my boss. He called didn't know it was my boss he was calling but he did, just to verify the terms. He never let on that he thought John was going to stiff him.

I listened for a few minutes then I really fell asleep. Later that evening I called Mr. Rocco and he said, I did good by sending him this deal. So he made me the managing partner to be the intermediary between the family and John, go figure.

The next day, that was the third day the attorney had the papers drawn up and the family sent over a Pullman full of cash and took the papers. The attorney verified the cash and gave John a cashiers check for the buy out."

Roscoe looked confused and said, "Lou listen I been listening to you attentively but you just lost me on that transaction. Now how did it work?"

Lou responded and said, "Look smart guy it was simple. I, Fred, I for Fred sold his interest to the mob at a premium because the arena project wasn't finished and he could not prove that they were going to make money eventhough they knew they would. So john was entitled to share in the premium from the sale. The goodfellas paid in cash so they got a discount on Fred's price and I got a little something, something out of that plus all I could take out of John's pocket until the bosses decided to get rid of him and keep it all for themselves. I would continue to get a small share until they got rid of me too but that is another story. So now you got it?"

Now it's the fifth day, the lawyers happy he got his fee, the family is happy there is some cash in the estate, John is happy he got a nice check and unbeknownst to him some new partners because he is under the impression that Fred was selling his share to him and the check he had just gotten was an advance. Little did he know?

Fred's Fatal Accident

Lou paused for a minute and started to laugh, Roscoe looking confused said, "What's so funny?" And Lou smiled and said, "I was thinking about the look on the maid's face that last night when I hide behind the curtains in the bedroom and she and the police came rushing in to arrest me. I mean the house was so big it was little a mansion it had I guess 20 rooms and every room had its own bathroom. The wine cellar was huge, it was like going into the liquor store.

So what happened was, I was in the bathroom around 10:00 o'clock that last night and I could hear people talking in the hallway. I couldn't hear exactly what was being said, but I knew that conversations in the hallway that late at night was unusual and I knew time was about to run out, so I slipped into the next bedroom, opened its door slightly and the stepped back and hide behind the drapes. That was when I heard the cops, the son and the maid burst into the bedroom looking for me.

After a minute or so they continued on looking through the house when the dust finally settled down and they weren't sure if there was someone pretending to be him or that he had actually lost his mind. I mean it was hours before they became convinced that either he wad lost his memory or that there was an imposter in the mix."

Roscoe said, "Man that is amazing, so what did you finally do?"

Lou said, "Eventually I was able to slip down

The DEADLY MAILMAN

stairs into the wine cellar and call John to come and pick me up that morning just before the second wave of searches were launched. What was surprising was when I called John, it had to be around daybreak, he got to the house within a minute. I couldn't figure that out. I know no one called him and told him about what had happened that night, the cops had literally just left. It could not had been 30 minutes earlier. I mean I waited until I thought the coast was clear before I called him.

But what had happened was John had already come to the house around midnight to make the switch and get me out and he saw the police car. He must have figured something was up so he waited down the street until the cops left. That was just after the old guy, Fred had taken a sleeping pill and laid down to get some rest. The son and the rest of the family had also left with the doctor. So at 4:00am it was only the maid and the old man left in the house. Even the chauffeur had left for the night. Somehow John made his way into the house and he must have went up to the old guy's room; I guess he was looking for me and found himself face to face with the old man."

John confronts Fred in the bedroom

The DEADLY MAILMAN

As soon as John walked up the back butlers staircase and stepped into Fred's bedroom he knew something wasn't right. John had expected Lou to be sitting by the window dressed and ready to go but there was Fred just about to doze off to sleep.

When John stepped into the room the light from the hallway shined right into Fred's partially closed eyes and he woke right up. When John called Lou's name and said, "Lou let's go, come on." Fred must have realized that his suspicions were now confirmed and he knew who had tied him up and locked him in the wine cellar for the last five days. It was his partner John Mason. As soon as Fred recognized the voice and realized what was about to transpired he jumped up out of the bed and immediately confronted John. John now startled realized that he hadn't walked in on a sleeping Lou but an alert and angry Fred.

Fred immediately told John he was quite aware of the kidnapping and that he was going to have him arrested and sent to prison. He said, he knew what John had did while he was being held captive and that he had already set things in motion to undo his scheme.

John was speechless at first but when Fred

went back to the bed to grab house phone John snapped and went into full battle mode. John rushed up behind Fred and pushed him down as he lifted the phone receiver. Fred was a tough old bird and he rolled over to the rooms seating area and went to open his lamp table drawer where he kept a small handgun. By then John had recovered and leaped over and grabbed Fred as he pulled the drawer open and saw the handgun. John shoved him in the back so hard Fred almost crashed through the floor to ceiling bay like window. Then John began to wrestle with Fred and the men began to through punches.

Before John knew what was going on the two men were out in the hallway tussling and then it happened, Fred pulled away and tumbled down the 18 step stairway and landed face down in a pool of blood. It seemed that several of the staircase's wooden railing spindles broke and one lounged in Fred's chest as he took the long tumble down the staircase.

While John didn't go down to check for a pulse on Fred's mangled body he did go back into the bedroom to straighten it up and make sure there were no signs of a struggle. It took him a few minutes to reposition the furniture and take the handgun and some jewelry just in case the police figure out there was a struggle, now they would think it was a burglar and Fred woke up and chased after him and fell down the stairs.

Then he just took the butlers back staircase down to the wine cellar where he had figured Lou would be waiting.

Lou continued: "Well the long and short of it was John had confronted the old man about the bonus he received from the sale of the stock. Somehow John figured out, if he was trying to get the old man to sell him his share of the business how did he wind up collecting a check. It should have been him paying the old man for his shares. The old man told him that he had sold a few shares to a third party and in order to maintain his rightful percentage of the company he sold some of John's shares and that was the reason for the payout to him. John didn't want to stay in the same position as a stock holder he felt that he should have wound up in a better position because the old man had sold off his edge. They got into an argument eventhough John had had me sign the papers to get take that particular option the old man over the stock away and give it to John. The lawyer had bamboozled him buy processing the old man's stock sale before he processed the power of attorney the old man had over the sale of the corporate stock. Anyway the old man took a header down the spiral staircase in the grand foyer and John needed to get me out of there before I was discovered and the whole scam blew up in his face."

Then Lou continued and said, "So here I am ready to be switched out and the mark had called the police and they were on the hunt for me, me hiding in plain sight just in time for this guy to stop by and kill the mark and get me out of there, go figure. Luck I say."

Roscoe started to scratch his head and said, "Sounds like a hell of an adventure, man."

Then Lou said, "Adventure that wasn't the half of it, man. This fool, John, didn't even tell me what he had done, as if it wasn't going to come out. I guess he felt that if an investigation was launched that the motive and opportunity would lead back to me. I mean my fingerprints were all over the place, so he thought. But I'll get back to that. That was when I realized what kind of a guy this John fella really was. You know I was glad I had switched the name of his beneficiary cause this was definitely the kind of guy who would try to stiff you. Oh yea! The fingerprint issue; I remembered when I went it would be better to be careful then sorry, so I used wax to mask my prints. I watched what I touched and when but you know it wasn't or isn't hard to keep up with what you touch when your on bed rest. My whereabouts were pretty much limited to the bed, bedroom and the bath room. So between the wax on my fingers and a few face cloths each night after everyone went to bed. I think I did a pretty good job."

CHAPTER 3

THE CORNER BARBER SHOP

Search

Later that morning the maid discovers Fred Beckett's body sprawled in the front door foyer and calls the police.

John Mason Office

Lou Gallo and John Mason were in a meeting when John's secretary came in and gave him the news that his long time partner Fred Beckett had fallen down a flight of stairs and died. John immediately cancelled the meeting and left to see what if anything he could do.

Up until that point in the meeting John and Lou had discussed Lou's first assignment. John had explained to Lou that Mr. Scurvy the owner of a well known barber shop on the corner of Atlantic Avenue and 7th Avenue in Brooklyn

Was a key location. John told Lou that over the past three years he had approached Mr. Scurvy several times about selling his shop and that he had offered him a substantial amount of money for it, however he refused to sell.

John told Lou that he plans on approaching Mr. Scurvy again to make him a cash offer right in front of his wife. And that might give him the leverage he needed to force him to sell. Lou said, "just because you make me an offer in front of my wife does not mean you are going to garner any leverage with me, more than likely you are just gonna piss me off."

John responded and said, "Of course that is the whole purpose because I'm not worried about him getting pissed off I'm hoping his wife gets pissed off." Then Lou said, "Why's that?" John responded and said, "I'm gonna give him 24 hours to accept the deal if he doesn't then you'll deliver these photo's of my friend Scurvy and this prostitute, along with this dummy summons's and complaint to appear in family court for a paternity hearing. That should push him over the edge. I'll just need you to deliver this to both him and his wife."

Lou smiled and said, "And if that doesn't work?" John sat back and said, "Then maybe a bullet to the head will help him get the point. The wife will already know that she can get cash when he's gone and that might be motivation enough."

Beckett's Residence Crime Scene

Nassau County Homicide Detective Sergeant Peter Miller, Fred Beckett's son Jason, the maid Loula and the Beckett family doctor, Dr. Jeffrey Kruta were standing in the foyer when John Mason walked in.

Det. Miller looked at John when he stepped and said, "Who are you? And what do you want here?" Jason Beckett said, "That is John he is like family around here." Det. Miller said, "What is your name?" Jason said, "Jason, Jason Beckett." Det. Miller shuck his head yes and said, "Right, right you are the victims son. So your name isn't 'Who are you' is it?" then he turned back to John and said, "Like I said, "Who are you? And what are you doing here?"

John said, "I am John Mason, a friend of the family and the victims business partner. So who are you?"

Det. Miller looked down at John and then turned to Dr. Kurta and said, "We got a comedian here doc. Tell me was your patient inclined to stumbling down a flight of stairs in the middle of the night?" Dr. Kurta smiled and said, "If you are asking whether or not this is a first time occurrence I would have to say yes. I have cared for this man for almost 30 years and always found him of good physical health and capable of negotiating this flight of stairs without incident."

Det. Miller then looked at John again and said, "So why are you here?"

John said, "I heard there was an accident and Fred was dead, so I came by to offer my support."

Det. Miller pulled out his note pad and started to make some notes after a moment he stopped and put the note pad away and said to the group, "I'm gonna need all of your contact information, I may have some questions after the medical examiner examines the body. Please see the officer on your way outside, thanks."

Jason looked at Det. Miller and said, "Is that it? Aren't you gonna, look into something, check for fingerprints, examine the body or something?" Det. Miller smiled and said, "Son why don't you just calm down and let the professional's handle this. The Medical Examiner will be here any minute and he will determine if there has been any foul play a foot son. Just calm down, ok? Good."

Jason looked at everyone and then turned to Det. Miller and said, "Obviously you believe this is some kind of a joke so I'll just step back and let you do what you feel is best. Will you need me anymore?"

Det. Miller smiled and said, "Not right now but I'll keep in touch. For your information at this point there isn't a whole lot to go on. We have a victim of what seems to be a slip and fall. No forced entry or break in, nothing missing. Until the medical examiner takes a look there isn't a whole lot to be said, right now." Jason said, "I'm just told you that my father has lived here for over 10 years there is no way he would miss-step on this stairwell and fall this hard to his death. Just the other day he was complaining that someone had kidnapped him and held him against his will in the wine cellar while we were being duped or being set up to be duped. Maybe it was them?"

Det. Miller said, "Son we been over that, three times in the last two hours even your fathers own doctor is no longer convinced of that and he was a strong supporter up until the third time we went over it. I mean even you had to admit you don't have any real evidence of such a conspiracy taking place. And like I said, until the M.E. takes a look we are just speculating."

At that point the Medical Examiners van pulled up.

Later that evening at 7th Avenue Barbershop

Seated in the last barbers chair with his feet up, watching a wall mounted big screen television was Sam Scurvy a tall heavy set balding black man with a loud laugh. When John Mason walked in the place was seemed rather relaxed. There were several people sitting around and two men cutting hair. The place was bright and clean and spacious looking. From the street between the large front windows and the full mirrored walls you could see everything and everyone in the shop. The front windows were floor to ceiling about 15 feet high and stretched the width of the building. The floor was covered in black and white extra large titles which matched the overall color scheme in the shop, that of an old time barbershop.

Everyone was talking and laughing but when John walked in everything seemed to get quiet.

The DEADLY MAILMAN

John being the first white man anyone had seen in the shop in a long time.

As the chatter subsided Big Sam the owner, suspected something was wrong so he draw his attention right down the middle isle of the shop and looked right into John Mason's eyes as he approached. Big Sam sat up and said, "Well what brings you here?"

John smiled and extended his hand in friendship and reached out and then over to get the TV remote and repeated his statement, "So what brings you here, Mr. Wannabe Developer and Parking Lot King?"

John smiled and put his hand in his pocket and pulled out a business card and wrote something on its back and gave it to Sam. When Sam took it and looked at the back of the card he said, "So what is this, a note from your mother about a hair cut?" People sitting around started to giggle.

John said, "That is an all cash offer for your little comedy club here and it good for 48 hours only."

Sam looked at it and then tore it in half and through it on the floor in front of John. As John bent over to pick up the pieces Sam said, "I done told you before I ain't interested in selling this place. When are you gonna get the hint?"

Just them Mable Big Sam's wife walked in and saw John pick up the pieces of card. Mable walked up and kissed Big Sam on the cheek and said, "Who is he?"

Big Sam said, "He was just leaving. We don't cut white heads around here, they do that on the other side of Brooklyn."

John smiled and said, "I was making your husband a very lucrative offer on this place, all cash, too. Maybe he should have asked you before he blew me off?" then he handed her the two pieces of card and turned and walked towards the door. When John got to the door he said, "That offer is only good for 48 hours Mrs. Sam. Just 48 hours" and he walked out.

Mable started to put the pieces of the card together and Big Sam said, "No need in you looking at that piece of paper and getting yourself all worked up over it, we ain't selling to his crooked ass or anyone. I built this business up and we are staying here until I die."

Mable finally got the two pieces of card together just well enough to see what John's cash offer was. When she saw he had offer Big Sam $750,000.00 she looked up at him and said, "That is a nice offer. What the hell is wrong with you?"

Sam reached into her hands and said, "Like I said, I built this business up and I ain't selling nothing until I die. I told you don't get yourself all worked up over nothing."

Mable got up into Sam's face and strongly whispered into his ear, "$750,000.00 in cash is a lot of money. No taxes. Just take the money and we can go away, retire. You can cut hair on the side out of the garage like you used to do. Are you crazy. Take it Sam before its too late."

Big Sam said, "That crazy ass white man done gone and upset my peace." Then he yelled out, "If that son of a gun steps his crazy white behind in here again, through him the heck out before I get my gun and shot him." A dead silence hovered over the shop for a moment. Then Mable said, "You ain't gonna do no such thing so stop saying things like that. And you better start thinking about taking that man's offer. He said, 48 hours and in 48 hours you better becoming with my share cause I'm willing to sell." Then she turned and started to walk back out. Big Sam grabbed her arm and pulled her close and said into her ear, "Woman don't play with me. I said we ain't selling and we ain't selling."

Mable pulled away and snatched her arm loose and then said, "Like I said, you need to be giving that offer some serious thought. This ain't about you. And I want my half" then she stormed out of the shop.

The Next morning at Big Sam's Home in Kew Gardens, Queens

Walking up the walk way to Big Sam's 2 story 4 bedroom Tudor style home as his wife Mable walked out to her car to go to work was the mailman.

As the two passed the mail man said, "I'm gonna need a signature mame." Mable stopped and said, "Who is it for?" The Mailman fumbled with the envelope for a second and then said, "It looks like legal papers I'm not sure." Mable said, "Legal papers, let me see that." The Mailman said, "Only if you are willing to sign for it?" Mable pulled her pocketbook off of her shoulder and said, "Well I understand, let me get a pen..." Mable found a pen and signed the Mailman's clipboard and he handed her the overnight envelope and walked away.

Mable continued to walk towards her car as she opened the envelope and what a surprise it was when she looked inside and saw the naked photo's of Big Sam and this Asian looking woman. Then she saw the summons and complaint demanding Big Sam's appearance in Family Court to determine paternity for the woman's two year old son named Samuel the III.

If Mable's head was a bottle cap it would have blown sky high. She couldn't get back to the house fast enough to deliver the bad news and to give Big Sam a piece of her mind.

As Lou waited at the end of the block to see if any thing would happen, after about an hour and a half Mable stormed out of the house with a suitcase and a bible under her arm. Big Sam followed her to the edge of the walkway, yelling and flailing his arms in the air. Mable just deliberately walked to her car, got in and sped off down the street.

Lou started his car and began to pull off when his cellphone rang, it was John Mason. Lou answered it and John simply said, "I got a call from the wife, she is coming over to sign over her half of the building. As soon as I get this notarized you can finish the job" then he hung up.

12:00 noon the next day in front of 7th Avenue Barbershop

The shop was full with barbers and customers alike. It was Saturday afternoon and everyone was trying to get their heads right for Easter Sunday. Holy Saturday is one of four of the busiest Saturday's of the year. And this year was no exception. It was a warm sunny late April Saturday and the shop had already brought in several thousand dollars and it wasn't even lunchtime yet.

Several of the local walking vendors had set up tables out front selling video's, CD's, incents and jewelry. As a afternoon mail mini truck pulled up across the street you could see that Big Sam was standing next to his barbers chair with his .38 in his belt making sure nothing went wrong with the cash on hand when the sound of breaking glass and people screaming rang out.

That was when the mail truck that was parked across the street quickly pulled away. The crush of people ducking and diving to the floor caused mass confusion in the shop and just outside the shop as well. No one could see what had or was happening. When things quieted down Steve the shop Manager shouted, "Somebody call 9-1-1 Sam's been shot, it looks like he's dead."

As one of the patrons dialed 9-1-1 another mini mail truck pulled up.

Lou pulled his mini mail truck around the corner and down the street and parked. He went inside the corner Dunkin Donuts shop and sponged a free decaf coffee off of them while he made a call to John Mason. The call was short and simple. Lou said, "It's time to meet, settle up and plan out the next project. I'll see you in the morning." And he hung up.

CHAPTER 4

THE SHOPPING STRIP

Work

A.J. Peterson and James Wallace have been friends for over 40 years and partners in a six store shopping strip located at the corner of Dean Street and 3rd Avenue just off of Boerum Hill for the last 15 years. A.J. a widower with a 25 year junkie son named Daniel lives in the Park Slope area of Brooklyn. James a retired police detective is divorced and lives just of the White Stone Bridge in College Point.

The two partners have had a rather subdued business relationship up until the moment John Mason visited them at their shopping center and proposed to by it for cash and a note in the neighborhood of $2,500,000.00 late last year.

A.J. was very interested in the offer but James didn't feel the timing was just right. James believed if they waited another 24 months the value of the property might go up to over $4 million dollars and then it would be time to cash out.

The DEADLY MAILMAN

Over the last six months John had stopped by on and off about six times almost once a month, stuck on the same offer amount.

This put a strain on A.J.'s and James relationship. A.J's primary motivation was retirement. He wanted to bank role his son and walk away, maybe go south and just lay in the sun until it was all over. James on the other hand didn't believe that A.J.'s son Daniel was ever going to make anything of himself other than a money sucking dope addict. James knew he could use the money as well but he was willing to wait to pick up an additional three quarters of a million dollars.

No sooner than John Mason started coming around and stirring up A.J.'s dreams of retiring did a little Gentlemen's club stripper named Pat Moore come into James life. James wasn't a stranger to the weekend five or ten dollar lap dance and he liked a good time but he was on a self inflicted pre-retirement budget, so he was very careful not to over indulge himself during these weekend excursions to the Gentlemen's club.

James and Pat eventually became an item and Pat even gave up Pole Dancing to spend more time with James and his newest venture inventing health drinks. James had made a few dollars in the sports drink development business in the past and recently he had picked up the sports drink crafting bug again, which excited Pat.

John and Lou meet about the Dean Street Shopping Strip

Within hours of the death of Big Sam Scurvy the barber Lou Gallo and John Mason were inside John's office discussing the next acquisition, the Dean Street Shopping Strip.

Lou shook his head 'no' and said, "What are you crazy? Before you start laying out any new projects or deliveries for me you need to square up on the last project. So you got my money in the wall safe or the safe deposit box?" John said, "Well it's a little tight right now I just paid out $350 large and I am on the hook for another $350 large any minute now." Lou looked at him and said, "So what? That ain't m problem. That is your problem and I expect it to be solved by tonight. Is that clear?" John stood up from behind his desk and barked down at Lou, saying, "You will get your money as soon as I can get it to you and not a minute sooner."

The DEADLY MAILMAN

Lou stood up and turned to walk toward the office, when he got there he turned and said, "I'll be back at 7:00 o'clock and you'd better have my $50 large." Then he opened the door and slammed it behind him.

John slumped back down in his chair and put his head in his hands and then started pounding on his desk. About 10 minutes later John's secretary opened the office door and said, "Det. Peter Miller, Nassau County PD is here about Fred Beckett." John looked up and said, "Tell him I'm in a meeting and to come back later."

That was when Det. Miller and his partner Det. Glory Watts pushed passed his secretary and walked up to the desk and sat down.

Det. Miller introduced him by saying, "Hello I'm Det. Peter Miller and this is my partner Det. Glory Watts and you are who?" John looked up and said, "Detectives I am really very busy preparing for a meeting I just can't talk to you right now, so if you will excuse me you can make an appointment with my secretary. I'm sure my calendar has some opening for this time next week." Then he got up and acted as if he was showing the detectives to the door. By the time he got to the door he realized that neither of the two detectives had moved, so he turned around and looked back at them and said, "Look I really don't have time for this, what is it that you want?".

Det. Miller looked at Det. Watts and smiled and then said, "You owe me lunch. Now Mr. Mason we have a few questions for you about your dead partner. Where were you the night he died? And what can you tell us about your relationship with the deceased?"

John walked back over and sat behind his desk and said, "The night of Fred's accident I was home. I had stopped by earlier and spent as much time as I could with him. The attorney was there. We discussed the signatory on our retirement account and our investment accounts. At that time I was signing as a secondary signature now I sign as a primary, one or the other. Look me and Fred were good friends as well as business partners. The man got me started in this business and it has been very good to me over the years. I'm really sorry to see him go."

Det. Miller smiled and said, "Oh! Really? We understand that while your friend and business partner was considered vegetating away you had your accountant and business lawyer come in and make some significant changes to the control of certain business assets in preparation for his demise." John sat back and said, "I beg your pardon, we made some precautionary changes due to Fred's deteriorating mental state not the state of his health."

Det. Miller then said, "Mental health, physical health the bottom-line is you move the balance of power just far enough to your side of the table to render any possible concerns for change away from your partners estate executor, thereby giving yourself full control, or so it may seem."

Looking surprise John said, "What are you talking about? Everything we did or I did was on the up and up." Det.'s Miller and Watts stood up and started to walk towards the office door. As det. Miller walked he said, "You say on the up and up, what does your partner say?" John smiled and said, "My partner isn't saying anything, he's dead, what you forgot?"

Det. Miller smiled and said, "I didn't forget anything but Eddie 'Pots and Pans' Rocco and his associates may feel differently when they get around to coming by to check the books, I dare say."

John now looking bewildered and confused said, "You saying my friend, my partner Fred screwed me?" Det. Miller reached for the office door and opened it and as they walked out he said, "I wouldn't say he screwed you I would say he just hedged his beat that's all. Or you could say he reduced his exposure to you, just in the nick of time. Oh! By the way, the M.E. sent us his preliminary report this morning and it said cause of death the result of a physical confrontation at the head of the stairs, it's a homicide now. Oh! Yea! We'll be back..." And they walked out.

7:00pm that night rear parking lot of the Cattlemen's Club

John Mason is hurrying to his 2013 black on black Mercedes 550 SL. When he hits the remote and reaches for the door handle two shots ring out, one hitting the drivers side passenger window and the other the drivers side of the rear window, neither window breaks but they both crack.

John attempts to duck and cover at the same time running over behind a dark blue Chevy Malibu parked next to his Benz. The shooting stops and John skiddishly peaks out over the car he was hiding behind over at his car and he see's Lou Gallo standing there with his gun still in his hand.

John sheepishly stands up with his hands out in front of him asking Lou what was wrong, why was he trying to kill him.

Lou smiled and said, "Look if I was trying to kill you, you'd be dead, right about now. Where is my money?" John started to say, I told you my situation this morning but he stopped himself when he notice Lou raising his gun barrel at him again and he said, "In the office safe, we can go and pick it up right now. I'll just have to work something out with the Widow Scurvy tomorrow morning." Lou lowered his gun and said, "You should have just said that this morning and your rear and back windows would still be like new."

John said, "Let me apologize for misunderstanding our relationship this won't happen again." Lou said, "You got that right, I operate cash and carry, only. That's why I call in advance for pick up after I deliver on my obligation. We clear?"

John said, "We are clear."

The DEADLY MAILMAN

8:00pm Back at John Mason Office

John opened his wall safe while Lou stood right beside him with his hand on his gun and the gun stuck in John's ribs. When John handed Lou his money he immediately closed the safe. John waved him over to the front of his desk and told him to sit down while he sat behind the desk in john's seat. Lou kicked back in John's desk chair after he counted his money and laid his gun on the desk in front of himself.

John looked at him and said, "Are you comfortable? We need to talk about the Dean Street Shopping Strip. What's your plan?" Lou said, "I got no plan, all the planning is up to you. I just deliver the message and by the way, I got a message for you, but not now, remind me before I leave to give it to you. So what's the plan?"

John tells Lou that right now he has one of the owners son's dealer in his pocket so if the owner doesn't want to sign his share over his son will get a hot shot the next day then he'll know I mean business." Lou said, "And that's supposed to make him do what? Bury his son? Lose focus on the deal? What exactly?" John said, "You tell me what, then. I said, I had a plan I didn't say it was a good plan."

Lou said, "I can see you long on ideas and short on planning ahead, here. Listen why don't I just care of this one and I'll call you within the week, just have my money on time this time. How much did you offer these guy's?" John responded and said, "I offered them $2.5 million dollars." Lou said, "Is that all cash or what?" John said, "No some cash and a short term note. I told them I could liquidate the note in less then 90 days once they sign. I can scrap up about $500 large in cash in 48 hours or so to make this happened."

Lou said, "How about I tell them you got $3 million in cash and they can have it in 24 hours or else." John said, "First or else what? Then how am I gonna come up with $3 mil?"

Lou smiled and said, "Or else I make another life changing delivery to them both and the son inherits the majority share and sells it to you for pennies on the dollar. Oh and that thing I was supposed to tell you about that I said remind to tell you later. It's now later. I'm sure your new partners would want to help you out of this financial jam that you are in, why don't you just ask them to loan you the $3 mil?"

John said, "That reminds me, I need to meet with these guy's, my new partners that is; face to face as soon as possible. This might not be the best way to introduce myself by asking for $3 million in cash to expand the business. What do you think?"

Lou smiled and said, "What you asking me? I don't know nothing. But you might want to think about that $3 million dollar request before you meet with them, just in case. I'll see if I can't work this Dean Street deal out before the weekend and we can talk more on Monday. Ok?"

A.J. Peterson's Park Slope Home-Saturday morning

Lou backs his official postal service mini van to the front door of A.J. Petersons house first thing Saturday morning and delivers four 3'x3'x3' boxes to his rear door.

Dressed in an official postal worker uniform, Lou knocks hard on A.J.'s rear door at 8:00am Saturday morning then steps back and waits for him to answer.

A.J. partially shaved wearing his bathrobe comes down stairs and looks out the front window and sees the postal mini van parked in his driveway, then he realizes it was the rear door bell that was rung so he goes to the rear door. When he gets to the rear door he looked out the doors window and he sees the four cardboard boxes stacked high on a hand truck and Lou in an official looking postal workers uniform so he opens the door. As the door opened Lou immediately started to push the hand truck with the boxes on it into the kitchen. Stepping out of the way A.J. asked who are you? And Lou said, "Where do you want me to leave these?" A.J. said, "Right there and what is this, who are you? You are not my regular mailman!"

Lou stood the boxes up near the kitchen table and handed A.J. a clipboard and said "I need a signature at the bottom. And Oh! Yea! I'm the special delivery courier, your regular guy should be here later this morning or when ever his scheduled time is. I just do special deliveries like this."

A.J. looked at the boxes and then said, "I didn't order any thing what is this stuff?" Lou pointed to the clipboard and said, "I don't pack'em I just deliver them" then he grabbed the clipboard back and started to shuffle papers on it and said, "Are you Mr. Smith? I see that these are computer set up's or something."

A.J. responded and said, "No, no there is no Smith here. You have the wrong address. Now please get this stuff out of my kitchen."

Lou grabbed the hand truck with one hand and then shoved the clipboard back into A.J. chest and said I need you to sign the bottom of the last page, so I don't get fired for being late in delivering this stuff to the wrong address. They will think I was goofing off instead of working." Frustrated A.J. said, "It's not my problem you people don't half know what you are doing over there," then he rifled through the clipboard and found the last page and scribbled his name on the bottom of the page and gave it back to Lou as he pushed the hand truck with the boxes to the kitchen door.

Once Lou had gotten behind A.J. he quickly turned and put his s&w .38 to the back of his head and fired two shots. A.J. fell to the floor dead. Then Lou walked over to the sink and washed the blood off of his gun hand and his face. Then he went over to the stack of boxes he had brought and pulled out a plastic sheet. Laid it down on the floor stood on it and began to undress. He carefully placed all of his clothes in one box and then took out another set and put it on, from his shoes and socks to his tee shirt and watch and I.D. badge. Then he reached in the bottom of the top box and pulled out a piece of paper and lightly dripped it in some of the blood that was on the kitchen table. Just enough to not soak it but to leave the impression that it was there and a trace of blood on the top of the sheet. He let that dry and then he picked up the plastic sheet, stuck it back in the cardboard box, and closed them up. Then he grabbed the dish towel he used to dry his hands to open the back door, put that in his back pocket and slipped out.

He walked around the front of the house looking to see if he saw any of the neighbors and he did, so as he approached the mini van he put the boxes inside and turned and waved good bye to A.J. purposively peering out the front door as he drove off.

James Wallace's House 9:00am

Then Lou hurried over to James Wallace's house. When he got there he parked the postal mini van right in front of the house, got out and hurried up to the door and rang the bell. Just as James opened the door Lou turned and started to run back towards the mini van. James looked at him and said, "Can I help you?" Lou turned slightly as he ran towards his mini van and said, "Are you James Wallace?" James said, "Yes! Why?" Lou continued towards the back of the mini van and opened the rear lift gate, peeked inside and then back around the side toward the house and yelled back, "I got some high value express packages for you, just give me one second." As Lou rifled through the letter baskets in the back of the van he looked around to see if anyone was on the street; seeing no one he leaned further into the mini van so far that he had to actually climb up inside of it.

After a minute James saw Lou stacking two 3'x3'x3' cardboard boxes on a hand truck and begin to roll it up the walk way. When Lou got to the open front door James was standing just inside holding the screen door which opened outward toward the right, open. Lou strategic placed the hand truck just inside the screen door so it would not close without him having to move the hand truck. He had his clipboard under his left arm, so when he placed the hand truck on the inside of the screen door towards the left of the door James was unable to see the handgun in the right hand side of his waistband because of the hand truck and the boxes on it.

Tﾑe DEADLY MAILMAN

Lou pulled the clipboard out from under his left arm with his left hand and held it up close to James' face, as he reached and pulled out his handgun.

When James realized that the name and address on the clipboard paper were not his he said, "I'm sorry but you have the wrong address but the right name."

That was when Lou stepped in between the hand truck and the screen door dropping his left hand with the clipboard still in it and placing the handgun in James' face. James immediately started to raise his hands and back up slowly.

James cautiously spoke and said, "What is this?"

Lou stepped inside the door and said, "Is there anyone else in the house?"

James thought for a second and said, "Yea my son why? What do you want?"

Lou said, "Ok! Into the kitchen and sit down."

James backed up and walked towards the kitchen. When the men had gotten into the kitchen James sat down at the table still holding his hands up. Then he said, "My son is probably calling the police right now, this really isn't going to work out well for you. You might as well leave now."

Lou smiled and said, "Oh! Really? Well if you had a son and if he was home, I might be concerned but that is not the case. And as for working out well? We'll just see about that. Now I have a question for you and there is only one chance to get it right. Otherwise we will see about that working out well or not question. Here is a sale of property acceptance. Don't mind the blood on it it's not yours, yet. It's your former partners, he chose not to sign. I guess his son will appreciate that better. Now if you sign it and I'll leave a check for you right now. Or?"

James said, "How much is the offer?" Lou said, "$2 mil." James said, "Hell no, last month it was $2.5 mil and we or I'm not even interested if it's last than $4.5 mil. So you can tell that little weasel Mason no deal."

Lou shot him in the left temple and dropped the gun on the kitchen table and picked up the unsigned offer letter from the table. Then he walked over to the kitchen sink, washed the blood off his arm and face went back to the front door, and carried in one box. He laid down his plastic mat, changed his clothes, picked up the mat, closed up the box, grabbed the wash cloth picked up the box and walked back to the front door. The he used the clipboard to close the door placed the box on the hand truck. Then he looked around to see if there were any witnesses and he pushed the hand truck back to the mini van, got in and slowly drove off.

Soon as Lou pulled around the corner from James house he called John masons cellphone. When John answered Lou said, "Something went wrong. Neither owner wanted to sign so it didn't go well for either of them. So what is your plan now?" John responded and said, "We'll have to have a chat with the son and the girlfriend. I pretty sure the son will cooperate the girlfriend she might make a stir but I'm sure we can handle that, worse case she can join her boyfriend in that great shopping strip in the sky." Both men laughed and then Lou said, "I'll be by for that payout in the morning." John said, "You're eating away at my working capital here. I'm gonna need a week to work that out." Lou responded and said, "You know I been working on my night aim, I don't think you find yourself in the same position you were in the other night do you? I told you I work on cash and carry, only. Pay up in the morning and we can hold off taking care of the other projects until you work out that cash flow problem, but I need my money tomorrow. Is that clear?"

John said, "Look I'm gonna need to take that up with my new partners tonight, one way or the other, but I'll take care of you tomorrow, so swing by around lunch." Then he hung up.

Across from Cobble Hill Park-Eddie 'Pots and Pans' Rocco Cousin Home

At 7:00pm that evening across the Cobble Hill Park in Brooklyn Congress Street, John Mason met with Eddie "Pots and Pans' Rocco his new business partner for the first time. The meeting was set up at Eddie's cousin's townhouse so that it would be convenient for everyone involved.

Inside the spacious modern Italian style duplex seated in the second floor library was Eddie 'Pots ad Pans' Rocco, his cousin Joe 'Two Thumbs Joe', their lawyer Murray Rosenberg and John Mason. Once everyone was introduced John thanked the men for meeting with him at such short notice but welcomed the opportunity to get to know them personally. Eddie spoke and said, "We have been meaning to stop in and chat but with the death and funeral in all we thought you should have some time to recover from your loss."

John acknowledge their sympathy and begin to talk about the parking lot business in general, but Joey interrupted him and said, "Not for nothing but we know a lot about the parking lot business, we own several in the Newark, New Jersey area so we are familiar with how you make your money. What we are interested in is your master plan for the new Barclay's Sports Center. Your now deceased partner, Fred was explaining that you were the driving force behind certain acquisitions that would add substantial value to our investment in the very near future. We would be interested in hearing more about that, now."

Looking over his oversized cognac snifter John immediately responded and said, "Yes we have some strategic ideas for that particular venue, however before we discuss those ideas I need to know what your plans are for this investment. I mean is this a short term venture or can I expect you to be around to enjoy the fruits of the labor. You see on the one hand once the expansion roles out there will be a substantial increase in the value of this business. Fred and I expected that the value of the business would have increased from $10 to $12 million dollars to about $15 million. But we project that the cash flow over the first five years after the expansion is complete to increase three to five fold, so after the first five years the value of the then seasoned investment would be worth between $20 to $25 million."

Joey spoke again and said, "We are long term investors, here. So what is weekly cash flow right now and what is going to be needed to get it up?" John said, "I like your enthusiasm. The weekly cash flow is about $50 large a week. And we have our eyes on four other properties in the immediate Sports Center area before we can begin converting and repurposing the properties we already have acquired in order to reap the full benefit of our planned expansion. Once all of the properties are in place and up and running the weekly cash flow should be a $125 large or more; more than double what we have now."

Joey smiled and said, "We'll send someone over to collect our share on Saturday morning around 10:00am." John smiled and said, "And what share do you think you will be collecting? I just told you we are in the midst of a major expansion plan, there is no shares to be collected. Every nickel is needed to build the war chest so we can pick up the last five properties.

Hell I haven't take a salary for the last six months. No there is no share until we complete the expansion and that is easily six months away. Sorry!"

Joey stood up and Eddie grabbed his arm and pulled back down. Then Eddie said, "No share?" John said, "Sorry we need every dime we can put our hands on to complete the expansion, what did Fred tell you guy's?"

Eddie said, "Fred never mentioned no share. No weekly collection. Now Mr. Rosenberg over there will confirm that. We don't invest like that. We don't even loan like that unless we are getting a majority interest and even then we collect weekly. Now how do you plan on making this right?"

John said, "Make what right? I didn't sell you any stock. I just meet you. It is what it is and I really don't know what to tell you. You invested and it is a risk you chose to take, win lose or draw. I'm sure Mr. Rosenberg over there will vouch for me on that."

Eddie looked at Mr. Rosenberg and Mr. Rosenberg shook his head no and looked away." John looked at Mr. Rosenberg and said, "You see." Rosenberg looked back at John and said, "I shuck my head no for you not for Mr. Eddie. You are the majority holder and you have a responsibility of making your investors happy. This is on you, sir."

John looked back at Eddie and Eddie said, "Listen before we get the wrong impression about what is or isn't going to happen with our investment let me say this. We have never, in almost 40 years lost on a loan or an investment. There is always a way. Sometimes the way gets clearer with the right kind of motivation, you listening to me, John. We think you might need some motivation to make sure that those weekly collections of $10 large are made on time. And I'm gonna have Mr. Rosenberg and Joey here come down first thing in the morning and check the books. You know like an audit. So we know how our investment is doing and verify the weekly collection amount. You hear me?"

John looks around and then he said, "So let's just agree that I hear you. There is one other thing I need to discuss with you." Eddie said, "Of course go ahead."

John said, "We are going to need to come up with some more money to pick up these other five properties over the next 5 or 6 weeks at the most. If we can raise it, then it will be about a year before we can actually start paying that money back. That will be when the properties are processed, converted and the Sports Center comes on line so we can generate the parking fees."

Eddie and Joey leaned forward and said, "So how much we gonna need?"

John leaned in and said, "About $3 mil."

Eddie looked at Joey and said, "So how much you gonna put in?"

John smiled and said, "I'm already all in and taped out."

Joey looked at Eddie and said, "We got $3 mil.?" Eddie said, "Last I checked we had it. That was this morning." Both men broke out laughing then Eddie looked at John and smiled a little grin and said, "So what are you willing to give up for this loan?"

John said, "Is it going to be a loan or investment?"

Eddie smiled and said, "What do you think?" John said, "I'm getting the feeling this would be a deal that will be an investment that will turn into a loan no matter what documentation I have."

Eddie looked at Joey and Rosenberg and said, "You see this guy is smarter than you two thought. I told you he would get it before he left here." Then he turned back to John and said, "So what's a little investment loan between friends. We got a deal?" John said, "What I am I agreeing to?" Eddie said, "We will make you a loan of $3 million dollars, to be drawn on as you need it. With interest payable weekly for one year and then lump sum payments on a monthly basis until it paid off. Let's say 3 years." John said, "So what is the rate and what will be the weekly payments?"

Eddie smiled and said, "Do you really care? I mean we are partners aren't we?"

John smiled and said, "I'm starting to get the feeling that being a partner with you is only healthy until you get what you want."

Eddie looked at Joey and said, "Who told you that?" then they both broke out laughing again.

John said, "Ok I think I need to think about this a little more before I answer you. Then he stood up and started to say good night to everyone.

The DEADLY MAILMAN

When he turned to leave Eddie said, "Don't forget tomorrow Mr. Rosenberg and Joey will be by to check the books and Saturday morning the weekly collections begin, a minimum of $10 large, we'll check the books again on Monday morning. You know it might be easier if we just send in a bookkeeper you know to help out."

John said, "I have a bookkeeper we don't need a bookkeeper and we can't afford another bookkeeper." Eddie looked at Joey and said, "Send that girl Patti down to see John in the morning, you know introduce them." Then he turned to John and said, "Consider that a favor. She's actually very bright girl, you know good with numbers. Keep an eye on her though." Joey looked at John and said, "Yea keep an eye on her, she's got sticky fingers." All three of the men broke out laughing as John smiled and walked out of the room.

CHAPTER 5

THE AUTO GARAGE

Visiting Hour

Next morning at 10:00am Lou steps off of the elevator at John Mason's office and walks right by his secretary and into his office. John's secretary hurries in behind him to let John know that she made an effort to stop him but there wasn't anything she could do. When Lou opened the office door he could she John hurrying to put his shirt in his pants and the woman who was with him was rushing around behind the desk straightening her form fitting dress.

Lou smiled and said, "Am I interrupting anything?" John turned around and smiled and said, "No come right in, I was just dictating some notes to my new bookkeeper, Patti. Patti meet Lou Gallo. Lou meet Patti."

Lou and Patti's eyes met and they both said, "Oh! Nice to meet you." John's secretary looked in over Lou's shoulder and said, "Mr. Mason I'm sorry there wasn't anything I could do." Then John said, "Not to worry Lou is like a partner around here, the door is always open to him, you can go back to your desk, thanks."

As the secretary closed the office door, John walked over to the wall safe but before he opened it he turned to Patti and said, "Patti, that will be all you can wait for me in your office. I'll check on you as soon as I finish with Mr. Gallo here. And welcome aboard." Patti picked up her pocketbook and slipped passed Lou and smiled.

Lou looked at her and grinned then he reached out and patted her on her bottom on her way out. John didn't see that but he heard it and as the door closed he said to Lou, "What the hell was that all about?"

Lou looking surprised walked over to the desk and sat down before he spoke. John opened the wall safe and pulled out $50 large and handed it to Lou as he went to sit behind his desk. As Lou counted the money John repeated his question and said, "What was that all about?"

Lou smiled and finished counting his money, when he finished he put it in his jacket pocket and said, "Let me give you a piece of friendly advice, you married?"

John said, "No why?" Then Lou said, "Banging

your partners spy is just asking for microwavable funeral, my friend." John looked at him and smiled then he said, "How did you know she was my new partners spy?" Lou said, "All in due time, my friend. Did they agree to the loan?" John said, "I'm not sure if I even want to take a loan from those guy's. I just don't understand them. On the one hand they seem like, likable people, and on the other they seem like loan sharks. I don't know. I'm not sure what to think."

Lou looked at him and said, "You're not sure what to think. What a surprise. Listen whose next on the list I got things to do."

John said, "I been after this auto shop on the corner of Bergen Street and Flatbush Ave. called Jose' Auto Repair. The owner, Jose' Cabrera and his son Hector have worked there for 20 years. I offered him about $1.5 mil. It's a big corner lot, they sell used cars there as well. He's turned me down each time I went by but his son seems eager. I think he wants out of the business. Right now I'm willing to take it off of their hands for $1.25 mil unexpected expenses you know. What do you think?"

Lou said, "Look I'll swing by there see if there is an update on the offer, give them the new figure and talk to them, see which way they want this to go. Maybe I'll bring them some discounted tools or something. You know the five finger discounted tools that might get them talking without feeling pressure, you know?"

Lou continued and said, "If it goes well then great, my fee will only be $25 large. If I have to motivate one of both my fee will be $25 large each. We good?"

John said, "It works for me. I hope it works out for them, its getting down to the wire; I've only got three weeks to secure acceptances before my guy leaves office and the whole roof is going to cave in. It will be like the Wild West in that neighborhood, prices will start to go through the roof."

John continued and said, "Now what's the story with you and Patti? Is there some history there you don't want me to know about?"

Lou stood up and said, "History, what you some kind of a comedian now? You got jokes? You a funny guy, right?"

John said, "No, no, I just wanted to know."

Lou walked to the office door and opened it

and said in a loud voice, "Watch that bookkeeper she's trouble" then he smiled a big smile towards Patti and walked to the elevator and left.

Lou Gallo's Insurance Office

Lou's insurance office was none dis-script, it was located right over the GWB between the Toll booths and the highway, on the fourth floor of the toll bridge plaza in New Jersey proper.

It was a one room office overlooking the buildings rear parking lot. It was quiet and simple in décor, most people would call it a mail drop with a desk, a phone and a window.

Lou stops by once a week to pick up mail, premium payments and the occasional beneficiary check that he quickly deposits into one of his many corporate accounts. Before the cash is actually put into his pocket he usually washes the money through four or five different accounts.

Lou places his occasional life insurance policy sale with one of four re-insurance brokerage firms in either New Jersey, Delaware, Pennsylvania or Maryland. That way no one firm gets to nosey about what he does or doesn't do as long as the premium payments are made on time.

Today Lou planned to swing by his insurance office sort through any checks that may have come in and then go and visit Jose and Hectors auto shop, but there was one piece of mail that he didn't expect. It was a notice of consolidation of all four of the small re-insurance companies he had dealt with over the last four years. It seemed that they were all being swallowed up by Nationwide Insurance Co. and in doing so a policy and practice audit was required. Nationwide wanted to schedule a onsite review of Lou's office, his books and records as well as his accounts to insurance that he was an acceptable independent agent and be allowed to continue placing policies with them. Additionally it would give the new re-insurer a solid handle on whether there were any fraudulent transactions in place.

Lou not only knew that this was going to end his insurance scam but that he might be facing some serious time; especially since he just placed that $1 million dollar policy on John Mason's life with a substantial upfront premium that he expected to be paid to him as the beneficiary with little or no questions.

Lou decided to ignore the notice for a few

weeks as if he was on vacation out of the country when it actually arrived, and he put it to the side on his desk.

Later that afternoon at Jose' Auto Repair Flatbush Ave.

Lou pulled up in a 1999 Ford Taurus sedan wearing an wrinkled postal couriers uniform. He engaged Hector first and asked him if he would take a look at the radiator and told him that the car was running hot and it was an emergency; he had to get to the station early for the night shift. Lou knew that a radiator job could result in a replacement of the radiator and the water pump and maybe a overnight storage fee.

While Hector fiddled around check the radiators pressure Lou engaged him in a discussion about retirement planning and pumped Hector up as having it good because he was in business for himself and could sock away plenty of cash for a rainy day.

Hector trying to keep Lou in the shop until he would have to call a cab to get to work on time leaving the car over night, opened up and told Lou that times were hard because of the economy and that he had a child on the way and felt trapped in a dead end job because his father owned every thing.

Lou went on and talked about the up coming Sports Center development and that a smart move might be to sell and get out.

Hector responded and said, "Well some guy had come by and offered them over a million dollars for the property but his father wasn't interested." Then he said, "... his father had put 20 years into the shop and wouldn't sell it for $3 million dollars."

Then Lou asked him, what if your father let you decide what to do, what would you do? Hector said, "I would sell this bitch in a heart beat." Lou smiled and said, "You know from time to time I come across used auto mechanic tools, my cousin sells them off of his truck, you know Snap-On and things like that. You interested if I can get you a good price?"

Hector said, "Hell yea! Man. But my father makes all of the purchases I just work on cars. If you could stop by in the evening he might take them off of your hands if you have the right ones." Lou smiled and said, "What would be a good time?" Hector said, "Come around closing that way the day's money will be in and he could make a decision right away. But when you gonna come by, I'm gonna need to keep your car over night, I can't get a radiator here until the morning." Lou looked at him and said, "Not a problem I'll just bring it back."

Hector looking dejected responded and said, "You sure you want to try to get home and then back here this thing could over heat again?" Lou said, "Oh! It will be alright it hasn't left me down yet. I'll be back with those tools, what about 8:00pm is that good?" Hector yea, but make it closer to 7:45pm in case it gets slow." Lou said, ok and he left in the car.

Nassau County Police Headquarters Detectives Squad

Around lunch time that same day Det. Miller called John and asked him to come down to their Mineola, Long Island Office to answer some questions about Fred Beckett's death and John agreed.

At 3:00pm John showed up with Jason Beckett his lawyer. Detectives Miller and Watts were dumbfounded to the two in the interrogation room. When Det. Miller walked in the first thing he said was, "What is this a joke? You two can't be serious. Mr. Beckett are you earnestly here to represent this man?"

Jason spoke and said, "Why not? How else am I gonna assure my client that his rights are being protected against any false allegations?"

Det. Miller said, "Number one if I have to get up and go speak to the D.A. about this I will and I am sure that you counselor will not be happy with the outcome. Number two just so we are clear, it is our job to follow establish procedure when it comes to investigating a homicide and interviewing all of the victims recent contacts is S.O.P. Now this is for you counselor, Mr. Mason here was asked to come down to help us in our investigation not defend himself as part of our investigation. All you presence does at this point is to make your client more of a person of interest when he may or may not earnestly be. Have I made myself clear?"

Jason stood up and picked up his briefcase and said, "I've already advised my client of his rights. I'll be outside if he has any questions. And I welcome a face to face with your D.A. have I made myself clear, detective?" then he walked out and closed the door behind him.

Then Det. Miller turned to John and said, "Mr. Mason we see that you had been a frequent visitor to the Beckett home over the week before Fred's death, can you explain why?"

John sat back and said, "That's wasn't unusual, we had been business partners for over 10 years almost 15, he was like a father to me. I told you people the last time you queried me, the man gave me my first start in business I owe him everything I have. Why wouldn't I be there every waking moment?"

Det. Miller smiled and said, "We understand that those waking moments were only focused around protecting the business from his family. Your accountant tells us that you had Fred agreed to giving you full signing authority on checks and loans. That doesn't sound very father son like, to me, how about you Det. Watts?"

Det. Watts smiled and shook her head no.

John said, "You people aren't going to make me out of the bad guy here, Fred was sicker than anyone ever thought, even the doctor can vouch for that. They didn't know if he was coming or going half the time. I had to do what I had to do to protect the business otherwise we could be tied up in court for years until this thing could be sorted out. Come on now."

Det. Miller continued and said, "You know John that would make sense and I could understand, but the way your accountant put it, it was like you had to get your long time partner to sign over the authority before the doctor even diagnosed the problem of this coming or going disease you call it. So I, no we began to wonder if the allegations that the man who signed those documents was really Mr. Beckett. I mean it seems as though you skillfully orchestrated the timing of this whole event. From the need for a check up, to the hospital stay, to the home bed rest to the signing and then the death. Do you agree?"

John looked at him and said, "Wow that sounds like a lot of planning for someone who can't seem to plan dinner at lunchtime. Get serious there is absolutely no benefit in my having my partner dead. Hell he's been carrying the business during this recent expansion program. If I have to cover the advances he made we'd be bankrupt."

Det. Miller looked at Det. Watts and said, "You

make a very good point about the repayment of business debts to the victims estate, however that is a mute point since the companies insurance would cover that and payout his heirs as well. We took a look at the policy you know. So your argument doesn't really hold water, but you knew that."

John sat back in his chair and said, "I don't know what you are talking about. All of our insurance and other inside financial transactions were done on the advice of counsel, so they are all legit."

Det. Miller responded and said, "On the advice of counsel you say? Which counsel? I mean you've got two that we know of and if you count your new partners counsel Mr. Rosenberg that would make three. Now I would guess that Mr. Rosenberg wasn't involved in that decision and it would go the same with Jason Beckett, a conflict of interest there; so who is this mystery legal eagle John? We need to verify your story."

John wiped his far head and said, "Maybe it wasn't advice from counsel but it is all on the up and up. Now I have some other pressing engagements."

Det. Miller stood up and said, "Well we do have a few more questions but they can wait. We'll keep you in the loop on our progress, especially our search for this mystery Fred Beckett look a like. Right now we are waiting for the FBI to get back to us about accessing their facial recognition software. They have national search capabilities. If we get through it won't be long until we track this imposter down. Then we'll have the whole story. You think?"

John stood up and walked towards the door and said, "Good luck with that detective, be sure to let me know how that works out for you." Then he walked out and closed the door behind himself.

Later that evening John stopped for an after dinner drink at the pub around the corner from his office. He couldn't get his regular table in the back room at the nudity show so while he nursed his vodka martini at the main bar he struck up a conversation with the Vince the bartender.

John was a little down realizing that more than likely he was going to have to make good on another $25 large payment to Lou in the morning and with out access to either Fred Beckett's deep pockets or the $3 million keyman insurance the company had taken out on Fred but was being held up because of the homicide investigation, he was quickly running out of working capital to complete the expansion plans. John knew he needed some relief. He figured he needed someone to replace Lou for more than the fact that he was bleeding him dry. He knew he could convince Lou to hold off the killing for cash and maybe take a piece of the action of delay the payoffs until every thing came together but more importantly if the police ever identified Lou and tied the two together John was going to go to jail for a long time for Fred's murder. So John knew he had more than one reason to replace Lou.

Vince engaged John in a conversation about making some extra money gambling on illegal street fighting. Vince said, "There was a after hours club not to far from the bar where they held street fights, members only. He asked John if he wanted to make a nice piece of money sponsoring him and betting on the fight he would show him where it was after closing. John asked him to explain what he meant by sponsorship and how much of a purse he could expect if he bet. Vince said, "The sponsorship is the entry fee for the fighter. Once inside the club owners matched up the fighters and the bouts were on.

The DEADLY MAILMAN

The winning fighter could win a minimum of $25 large to be split between him and his sponsor. The sponsorship fee is $5 large; the net to the sponsor was $10 plus their $5 back for $15 large and the fighter would get $10 large if he won. Otherwise the sponsor lost $5 large and the fighter got zip plus his ass wiped.

John said, "So how much is bet?" Vince said, "A good fight that went 3 full rounds probably $75 to $100 large to a smart better."

John said, "So what makes a better smart?"

Vince leaned over the bar and said, "First find a winner like me. Then sponsor him. In the first round bet $25 large to win on me. In the second bet $25 large against me. Then bet $50 large on a knock out by me. That way you pick up $10 large of my winnings, $25 large in the first round when I look good, $25 large in the second when I look bad, and $50 large in the third when I knock the fool out. For a total of $110 large and tip me $15 large for a net of $95 large in less than one hour. What do you say?" John said, "I gotta go get some cash and I'll meet you back here in the rear parking lot at 2:00am." Vince stuck out his hand and said, "Put it there partner." John shook his hand and said, "Let's see how this works out tonight. I'll let you know when we can talk about partnerships."

8:00pm at Jose' Auto Repair

Lou drove his 1998 Blue four door Volvo and to the shop and parked three parking spaces away from its Flatbush Ave. entrance. The property was a large corner lot with an office and 4 garage bays, seated in a diagonal manner to allow for vehicle access from both Flatbush Ave and 7th Ave. Access to the storage lot was available from both 7th Ave and Flatbush Ave. The business office was on the 7th Ave side, the farthest point from the Flatbush Ave side. The men's and women's public restrooms could only be accessed from the outside on the Flatbush Ave side of the building. The office, which was located on the 7th Ave side of the building, had 3 entrance doors; one in front of the building, another connecting the office to the service bay area, and the third along the back wall leading into the storage lot in the rear.

Carrying 3 plastic garbage bags Lou parked just about dusk and slowly walked along the Flatbush Ave fence line to the restrooms, where he slipped into the unlocked men's room. Inside the men's room Lou took a pair of rain pants and jacket out of one bag and put them on. Then out of the other bag he took out a black baseball cap, some rubber gloves and 2 smaller plastic bags. He put the 2 small plastic bags on his feet, the gloves on his hands and the cap on his head and slipped back out of the rest room door and slowly walked along the buildings rear wall. Since the rear parking lot was well organized his route to the office back door was unobstructed.

With all of the noise inside the bay areas it was impossible to hear Lou walking through the rear storage lot. When Lou came upon the open rear office door he could hear Jose talking to his son Hector.

Jose was telling Hector about the papers his accountant had him sign earlier in the day. Jose said, "Hector look those papers you signed earlier were to give you the same access as I have to all things that go on around here. The bank accounts, the loans papers, the mortgage, the utilities everything. I told you yesterday, Grand Pa was not doing to good and the doctors fear he may not have much more time. I have to go back to the D.R. tomorrow to see him. I am not sure if it will be for a few days or a few weeks. I don't know, he may want to come back here with me or go to Puerto Rico with your aunt Maria. I will know when I see him. But in the meantime you have to keep the business going. Things are going good and it should continue this way for the next few months at least. Our contract with the Parking Violations Bureau is paying off and business has picked up from our regular customers and the community as a whole."

Jose continued and said, "While I am gone, you should call up that school APEX and get a couple of interns to help out. They aren't going to cost us anything, maybe lunch and dinner and bus fare. You can give them $50 a week and they can keep all of their tips. Those guys are hungry to learn and they are good so maybe one of them will stick with us when they graduate."

Hector said, "Ok but you are coming back aren't you? You're starting to scare me Poppy."

Jose smiled and said, "You been working here for what 10 years and I have treated you like a kid and now I have to start treating you like a man, because I'm not always going to be here. I know I can trust you to do the right thing. So go on and close up I'm going home early to pack."

Hector smiled and said, "Thanks Poppy I got it. I'll hold down the business while you are away.

You just take care of Grand Pa."

Jose said, "Ok I love you son, see you when you get home."

Hector turned and walked toward the service area and said, "Love you too Pops." Then he turned around and walked back and hugged his father and then left.

Just as Hector walked into the bay area and the door closed behind him, Lou opened the rear office door, slipped in and walked up behind Jose and shot him in the back of the head. Jose' lifeless body fell to the floor and Lou pumped two more shots into his chest and walked back out the same way he came in. He back tracked through the rear storage lot and into the men's rest room again.

He took off the rain gear and the plastic bags from his shoes and placed them all back as they were when he came in along with the hand gun. Then he slowly walked back to his car and neatly placed the bags under a blanket in the truck of his car. Then Lou got into the car and drove into the lot of the repair shop.

As he pulled up Hector walked out to assuming he was a new customer, to tell him they were about to close. When Hector realized who it was he said, "What happened? Where is the Tarsus?" Lou put the car in park and stepped out and as he walked to the rear of the car he said, "I got those tools, is your father around?"

Hector stuck his chest out and said, "I got this, show what you got."

Lou opened the trunk and let Hector see all of the tools he had. Hector examined a couple of the tools and looked at them closely but he didn't see anything he needed so he turned and told Lou that he didn't see anything that he could use. But he recommended that Lou go across the street and try his competitor, that they might have use for them. Lou was disappointed but understanding he said, "The next time I get a set can I stop by?" Hector said, "Of course, but what about that Tarsus, when you gonna bring that back?"

Lou closed the trunk and as he got back into his car he said, "It's cooling off, if I can get it started tomorrow I'll come back by. Then I can see your competitor while you work on it." Hector said, "Ok! Try to get here before lunch, see ya."

As Lou turned his car around he could hear one

of the mechanics run out calling to Hector telling him to come and look, his father was dead.

Lower Manhattan Fight Club 3:00am

When John and Vince pulled up and got of their cab there was a line of cabs around the block letting couples under the single lamp post in front of the fight clubs entrance. John followed Vince into the rear door of one of the many cookie cutter type downtown pier warehouses, into what seemed to be Madison Square Gardens during the basketball playoffs. While this was New York City night life in still amazed John that so many people could fit into one place without having a parking lot as large as a football stadium outside.

Vince introduced John to the fight promoters Rick and Brad, twin brothers with heavy Russian accents. While they were twins they looked as if they were models for steroid magazine. The slick black hair and tight Italian made silk suits didn't help their image either.

John paid the entry fee and was told to make his way over to the bar and when Vince's fight was announced he could come up to the promoter's box, the mezzanine and watch. Vince explained that the promoters box was were the bets could be laid and the payoffs received.

John walked around and checked the place out while he waited for Vince's fight to start. He got a chance to see some of the fighters warm up and listen to what some of the spectators were saying. John didn't let himself get caught up in the fan-fair of what he called fight groupie's and violence junkies, but he did focus in on what people were saying about each of the fighter warm ups.

He was surprise to hear that everyone he walked by seemed to feel that Vince had good technique although he did not hear anyone say that they had seen him in the ring before.

Just before Vince's match was to begin John did hear some people comment that his opponent was their personal favorite. Between those comments and the seemingly up tick in the betting from the floor John grew more and more confident that there was money to be made in this particular match up.

Finally Rickie sent one of his security people to find and escort John up to the promoter's booth on the mezzanine.

The DEADLY MAILMAN

As John walked into the booth he recognized a number of faces however he could not recall any names. After about a minute the match was announced in the ring and the real betting began. A hostess approached John and asked if he wished to bet, John quickly bet as he was instructed by Vince, $25 large to win the round.

When the battle began, Vince was kicked in the head and knocked to the floor for a 5 count. Vince slowly recovered and returned the favor with a devastating body blow and a round house kick to the back of his opponents head, flooring him for a 3 count. The next five minutes of fighting was furriest with each fighter taking what anyone would call were eschews hating blows. At the end of the first round the referee called the bout a tie. John immediately rolled his bet over for the second round against Vince, which raised everyone's eyebrows in the promoter's booth. But John shrugged it off and jokingly said out loud, "hay I'm here to win it ain't personal."

The second round started off with the same kind of fireworks as the first did, with Vince's opponent knocking Vince to the floor for a long count this time. John was surprised to see Vince attempt to get back up but he succumbed to the body blows and drop kick, and stayed down for the count.

Now the crowd was in a frenzy, at the beginning of the third and final round. John didn't hastate when asked if he was interested in betting. He said, "That's exactly what we are here for right?" And he bet $50 large on Vince to win. When Rickie heard what john was willing to risk he walked over and to him and said, "This is your first time here isn't it?" John looked at him and said, "Why do you ask, does it show?" Rickie laughed and said, "Odds are your guy is not going to do well this round. Do you know something we don't?" John looked dead into Rickie's eyes and said, "I got another $50 large that say's I do." Rickie looked back at John and said, "I like a guy who will put his money where his mouth is. I'll take that bet." And then he walked back to his seat.

When the bell rung and Vince's opponent stood up to walk to the middle of the ring, Vince was slow to get up. By the time his opponent realized that Vince hadn't gotten off of his stool and the referee began to count him out in his seat, he had walked to the middle of the ring. As he took his last step Vince rushed head first at him. His opponent loaded up a hay maker, dropping his right shoulder and fist to upper cut

The DEADLY MAILMAN

Vince up on his approach. But Vince flipped half way there and came down with an elbow to the top of his opponents head knocking him to out.

The crowd went wild. In less than 10 seconds Vince went from maybe a new comer to a top contender and John from a possible $75 large winner to a $125 large winner and a respected gambler and promoter.

CHAPTER 6

THE LAUNDROMAT

Cell Search

The next morning at 10:00 am Lou Gallo shows up to John's office looking to get paid for the hit on Jose Cabrera. Lou was seated behind John's desk with Patti sitting in his lap when John walked in. John shocked but not surprised asked Patti to excuse them for a minute. Patti got up and straightened her skirt and hurried out of the office. John walked over to his desk chair and Lou politely got up and went and sat on the other side of the desk. As Lou flopped down in the side chair he said, "So what's your problem this morning? See something you didn't expect? Or were you up all night?"

John sat down and looked at Lou and said, "What's with you? You following me or something? And what the hell is with you and Patti there? You keep hinting that there is something there but you never say what?"

Lou smiled and said, "Let's take business first then we can reminisce." John sat back and said,

"I'm all tapped out right now. These properties are closing faster than I expected and every time I pay you I find myself getting shorter and shorter on working capital. I'm gonna need a few days to put your money together." Lou sat up and said, "We had this conversation a few days ago, did I agree to any changes in our relationship?" John said, "No but that doesn't change the fact that I am out of cash and it is going to take me a few days to put some money together for you, that's all."

Lou stood up and said, "Now we aren't communicating any longer. I just said, I need my money and you haven't made a move to hand it to me. Must I return to a more persuasive posture?" And he pulled out his .38.

John sat back again and said, "Look that worked the other day, but it is now clear to me that if you shot me, you definitely won't get paid and the cops will be here before you can get out of the parking lot. So that doesn't scare me."

Lou put his silencer on the barrel and John started to sweat but he didn't budge. Then Lou shot so close to john's head he blistered his earlobe. John jumped out of his seat and started screaming at Lou, Lou took aim again and John quickly calmed down. John repeated his lack of available cash to pay Lou with and Lou said, "Ok, ok I believe you. Give me your car keys."

John looking confused said, "What?" Lou said, "You heard me, give me your car keys." John reached into his pocket with one hand while he checked the blood from his lobe on the other hand. Then he pulled out the keys to his 2012 Mercedes Benz SL 500 and through them on the desk and said, "That is a $95,000 car, I only owe you what $25,000." Lou said, "I figure the car will be collateral for the next two jobs and if you don't come up with the cash before I finish them it will buy you 30 more days to pay me in full. Then I'll keep the car."

John said, "And what am I supposed to do?" Lou smiled and said, "I don't know, do dead men drive?" then he walked out.

John proceeded to put his fight winnings in the wall safe as soon as he finished in walked Mr. Rosenberg and Patti. Before John could even offer Mr. Rosenberg a seat, in her most adult voice Patti said, "Open the safe we are here for the weekly vig." Stunned John sat back and looked at the two of them and said, "You are here to what?" Patti said, "Did I stutter? Open the safe and hand me the books, we are here for the weekly vig. Get to it!"

John smiled and said, "Look, beautiful first off I explained to your boss or bosses there, there is no weekly vig. The cash flow is barely enough to keep the lights on while we continue to fund this expansion program. Besides, your share in the business is less than 10%. Who the hell are you to come in here throwing your weigh around? Tell Mr. Plates and Saucers or whatever his gangland name is, I'll call him when I need him. Now get out; both of you; out!"

Patti looked at Mr. Rosenberg and he nodded for her to leave. Then he turned towards the door and as he walked out he looked back and said, "John, I've been doing this a long, long time and I have never gone back with a message like this and it ended happily. You sure you don't want to reconsider?"

John stood up and said, "Is there some part of what I said, that wasn't clear?"

Mr. Rosenberg smiled and said, "No. you were clear. Have a nice day" and he closed the door behind him and left.

When the office door closed, john turned and

grabbed his chair and through it up against the wall then he turned and swept every thing off of his desk in one fell swoop with his fore arm.

He walked over to his window and peered out for a moment when the office door flew open. By the time John turned around to ask who it was, he found himself hanging upside down outside of his 4th floor office broken window.

With large chards of glass failing on each side of his head all he could was scream as he fell two and half stories to the canopy over the lobby entrance.

When he hit the rooftop he looked up and saw his secretary holding her head and screaming in horror as he laid there bleeding. Before he passed out he saw a man peer out of the window from behind his secretary wearing a black ski mask, black sweat shirt and black pants shout back, "We'll be back next for the money." Then he disappeared into the office.

Nassau County Police Headquarters—Homicide Detectives Squad Room

Seated around a small conference table in the Detective Captain Bullock's Office were: Detectives Miller and Watts, Jason Beckett and his law partner Retiring City Councilmen Mark Oliver and Captain Marvin Bullock.

Captain Bullock was on the telephone with Supervising U.S. Marshal Bertrum Cooke in the Marshal's Regional Office at Federal plaza in lower Manhattan.

Captain said, "Bert let me put you on speaker, you already know Det. Miller and Watts. Let me introduce Attorney Jason Beckett and his law partner and City Councilmen Mark Oliver..."

Captain Bullock laid out the situation as thoroughly as he could but Jason Beckett was compelled to emphasize selected aspects of the case which he felt required outside attention. Surprisingly Councilmen Oliver noted that, "...some might misconstrue his behind the scenes comments are throwing his weigh around in support of John Mason expansion efforts but his action were no more of less consistent with anything his colleagues had done in the passed or were currently doing." Captain Bullock excused himself from the conversation and the room for a few minutes after those comments but he did offer a disclaimer before he left.

Marshal Cooke asked Jason what would he

have him to do, acknowledging that he and captain Bullock had, had a great history together and that he certainly understood the budget constraints the Captain was currently faces which precipitated his reaching out for help from the Marshal's office.

Jason repeated his earlier statement that he felt no one was seriously considering the kidnapping complaint his father had leveled. Noting that the only who could have benefitted from such a scheme would be John Mason. Marshal Cooke agreed that, after talking with Captain Bullock and the other Detectives on the case that his concern could make the difference if a case could be made one way or the other. With that he told the group he would have one of his direct reports, a Marshal Harry Bailey initiate an independent investigation into the matter and report back to all concerned within two weeks. Marshal Cooke went on to say that at that point they would have to be willing to accept his findings and move forward from there. Jason and Mark agreed as did Detectives Miller and Watts.

Sunday morning --New York University Hospital Downtown Recovery Ward

Lou walked into John's private room carrying a

boutique of roses and a get well card. John looked from his bed and said, "What the hell do you want?"

Lou smiled and said, "Don't get mad at me, I wasn't the one who decided to take a flying leap out of a fourth floor office window because my business partner sent over a subtle reminder that the vig was due. I think you are an incredible lucky man. Usually things like this don't turn out so well."

John looked at him and said, "So what are you here to gloat?"

Lou said, "No, no! I was just wondering what you plan was for settling up with the Cabrera family auto shop. I mean the old man is dead and the son said, he was looking to move on for a price." John said, "If you haven't noticed I'm a little busted up right about now. Come back in a few years and see if I give a dawn."

Lou smiled and said, "Oh now you want to consider your dilemma. Let me put it to you this way. If you thought those guys over reacted when you told them no vig this week wait until they find out you scrapped the big payoff by deciding to walk away. That will make them real happy I assure you. John come on, pull your self together. You are in this until the end, which could be any day now with that kind of an attitude."

Lou said, "Look I got an idea, why don't you go borrow what you need from your new partners and pay them back quicker than they expect. You are probably going to have to give them a larger share of the business but that is better then being dead and them taking over all of the business isn't it?"

John sat up as best he could with two cracked ribs and said, "Look I'm giving those guys any more of my business and certainly am not going to keep them around as partners much longer either. But I am going to borrow some money from them to finish this expansion. I guess if I finish this and the business becomes all they think it could, they'll stake me in my next venture then we can make real money."

Lou said, "You got an idea that is going to make you and your partners some real money, once you finish the expansion of this business? What idea would that be?"

John smiled and said, "Now if I told you then it

would be your idea, wouldn't it?"

Lou said, "I'm not your partner nor am I the enemy, but have it your way. So who's next? I count we have three more to go and less than three weeks to get them done in."

John went on and said, "There is a Laundromat next to the auto shop you just visited. It's owned by some old bitty. She probably still has her first nickel in her hand bag; the old bat. The building isn't that big but it completes the corner and faces Flatbush Avenue which makes it very visible for the parking public. I offered her $500 large, last year and she laughed at me. She said it was worth a million if a dime. She maybe right but all I want to pay her is $500 large. I suggest you deliver a message to her through her elderly sister. She must be about a thousand years old herself as well. Get rid of her sister and she will have no reason to stay in New York. So she'll probably sell for $750 large."

Lou said, "Well if I take out the sister and the owner wants $570 large how you gonna pay that and me and the weekly vig?"

John said, "I said, I'm going to need a short term loan from my partners and the rest of this is a wrap."

Lou said, "I can say one thing for you, you got balls. I'll take care of that delivery on Wednesday and then I'll see you on Thursday." And he left.

Cobble Hill Park-Eddie 'Pots and Pans' Rocco Cousin Home

Later that evening John signed himself out of the hospital and went to visit Eddie 'Pots and Pan's" Rocco's cousins home on Cobble Hill Park.

John's cab pulled up, he told them to wait and he gingerly got out and went up to the ring the door bell. When the door opened and the guard began to search him he heard some tires screech off and he looked around and saw a black Mercedes Benz drive off around the corner, but he recognized that license plates as it drove off. It was his car.

So as he walked inside to the library he began to put two and two together and came up with four. When he walked into the library both Eddie, his cousin Joey, and Mr. Rosenberg were already seated and nursing some snifters of cognac.

With a loud voice Eddie welcomed John and asked him to have a seat, while Cousin Joey just sat and looked on with contempt. Mr. Rosenberg smiled and seemed to be very pleasant.

Eddie spoke first and said, "I'm surprised to see up and around you look terrible." Then he looked at Joey and Mr. Rosenberg and said, "Doesn't he look terrible? He looks like he should be lucky to be alive!"

John looked back at him and said, "It's nothing, just a little misunderstanding between business partners."

Eddie smiled and said, "Partners like that you gotta wonder."

John smiled and said, "Just a little getting to know each other."

Eddie looked back at John and said, "Do you think they now know each other?"

John said, "It seems clear to me. Now the question is whether its clear to them?"

Joey spoke and said, "And what is that suppose to mean?"

John said, "You take it the way you want too. It's clear to me what you guy's are capable of. But I don't think it's clear to you what I'm capable of."

Joey reached into his waistband for his gun. Eddie grabbed his hand and held it in place, then he said, "Calm down there, calm down, let the man speak."

At that point John had pulled a .25 automatic from a tourniquet that was around his left shoulder and pointed it at Mr. Rosenberg who put up both of his hands in surrender.

Eddie took his other hand and cautioned John to put the gun down.

John looked at Rosenberg and said, "No, no restitution is due. You people colluded with my former partner to screw me, then you try to bitch slap me by having some thug sneak attack me, after you tried to saddle me with some bookkeeping floozy? I ain't some High School drop out who got lucky here. I've been in this game a long time and I have had my share of second rate mobster like two. Now its time for restitution which one will it be? Cousin Joey or Mr. Rosenberg. You choose. Now!"

Eddie stuttered and slowly released and then moved his hand away from Cousin Joey's hand. At that second John fired into Joey's shoulder and then hit Mr. Rosenberg in the head. As Rosenberg slowly leaned over and hit the floor, Eddie yelled why did you do that? Why? He didn't have a gun."

John stood up and stepped over to Joey and put the gun against his left temple and said, "That is the problem with you people, you got no character. You can't keep your word. You got no integrity." Then the door swung open and it was the guard with his gun out. Eddie yelled no, no don't shot him. Don't shot him. Every one just relax. Let's just calm down."

John waved to the guard and said, "You put the gun on the floor, put your hands up and kick it over here. Or both of your bosses are going to take it in the head right in front of your eyes."

The guard looked at Eddie and Eddie said, "Do as he said."

The guard replied. Then John said to the guard lay down on the floor and face the wall." Eddie said, "My cousin here he is bleeding all over the place, he needs a doctor."

John looked at him and said, "The bullet went through he'll be alright besides I got more. Now let's get down to business. Don't think, don't ever think I'm the bitch here. I'm the majority partner and I expect to be treated with respect. The next there is a problem you can just imagine what might happen. I won't kill either of you this time, but don't think I'm ever going to be treated like some bitch on the street."

John continued and said, "Now take the guards shirt and stop the bleeding it's annoying me." Eddie took off his shirt and gave it to Joey to hold against the wound. Then John said, "I need some money to finish the expansion. I need $3 million. I'll pay you back $5 million one year after the Sports center is completed. I will pay $25 large a week starting one week after you give me the money, all cash. As an incentive, I will give you a 50% share of the business but when we sell the business after the third year of its operation the split will be 60%-40% in favor of me. We should be able to get in the neighborhood of $20 to $30 million for all properties in a bulk sale for that much. Now if that is acceptable. I have one more piece to this puzzle, a sweetener."

Eddie said, "I'm still listening and so is Joey."

I've already earmarked half of that $25 or $30 million to invest in small legitimate manufacturing company. Now that might not sound like a big deal to you guy's but think about this; the company has an exclusive patent on converting medical marijuana plants to tablet's. That's all I can tell you right now. If all of this works for you fine. If not fine. I already told you I'm not even taking a salary so that this expansion project can come to fruition. Your 10% is 10% you want out let me know and I'll find away to make it happen. The Lucci family is interested in the entire package as offered and they are willing to put in an additional $10 million just to make things go a little smoother. You let me know your decision in the morning. I'll be in my office at 10:00am sharp."

Eddie said, "I see you've thought this thing out. We'll think about it. I can't speak for Joey over here but if we agree then it will be what you say. If not then...what can I say? Right now we don't really have legal counsel so we will do the best we can before 10:00am; and by the way, we are going to want restitution as well, some day."

John started to back out of the room and as he did he said, "Funny thing about restitution as long as money can be made there will always be someone with a better offer or to get or pay restitution for a loss. Just because you see me standing here alone, never make the mistake that

I am alone." Then as he walked to the door Eddie said, "What are we supposed to do with Mr. Rosenberg here?"

John stepped over the guard and opened the library door and said, "That's your problem he should have been armed." Then he walked out and closed the door behind him.

Flatbush Avenue Laundromat

Clara Mosby was the owner of the Flatbush Avenue Laundromat. She had inherited it from her late husband William and had operated it for almost 20 years. Clara was a retired elementary school teacher and mother of one son Walter who lives in Florida. Every year Clara snow birds to Florida with her elderly sister Bernice to spend the harshest New York winter weeks with her son Walter.

Bernice, also a retired elementary school teacher lives alone not to far from the Laundromat and Clara visits and has lunch with her everyday. Clara checks on Bernice daily, tidies up for her, makes sure she eats, and takes her medicine. Then she returns to the Laundromat to finish up any folding orders she receives and closes the store in the evening. The Laundromat is open 24 hours a day, 7 days a week. Clara manages the shop most of the time but she has two part time workers who cover the late night and weekend shifts.

Shortly after relieved her night shift manager with only a few customers on the floor John Mason limped in carrying a small portfolio. Clara immediately recognized John from past experience so she already knew why he was there.

John limped up to the long folding counter where Clara was quietly sitting and folding a basket of linens and said, "Good morning Ms. Mosby how are you this fine morning?" Clara looked over her reading glasses and smiled, but she didn't say a word. Then John said, "I see you are busy so I won't take up much of your time. I wanted to stop by and give you an update on my earlier offer to buy this building. You haven't sold it yet have you?"

Clara looking over her reading glasses again looked down at the floor and said, "Does it look like someone else owns this place? You look a little beat up. Were you in a car accident?" John said, "No skiing. Sorry but I had to ask. I was wondering if you were still firm on rejecting my earlier offer of $500,000 all cash?"

Clara stood up and walked around to the back of the folding table and said, "If I told you, the last time you came up in here, that the price was $1 million dollar then why would I accept half of that now?"

John said, "Sorry but I had to ask. Can I offer you a little more?"

Clara responded and said, "If you are going to offer me a little more than a million dollars then I would be inclined to consider it but anything less would be a waste of your time."

Then John pulled out a pen and wrote a number on the back of one of his business cards and slide it over to her face down. Clara reached and picked it up; she looked at it and put it right back down and slide it back to him and said, "You need to go ask who ever it was that educated you to give you your money back, because they forgot to teach you how to listen. I said, one million or more not less. So if you don't have anything else to do please go do it somewhere else."

John picked up the card and wrote the date on the back of it then he pushed the card back towards her and said, "Three quarters of a million in cash no questions asked, no paperwork, no legal fees, and no taxes that's worth more than a million dollars right there. Do you understand?"

Clara did not respond. John continued and said, "Ok, not a problem, but if you ever change your mind please feel free to call me. That offer stands firm for the next two weeks though" then he turned and limped back out the door.

Clara Mosby sister Bernice home

Not far from Clara's Laundromat is the home of her elderly sister Bernice. At 10:30am that same day Clara called her sister Bernice as she usually did to check on her. The two women chatted about the weather for a few minutes and then Clara asked her what she wanted for lunch. Bernice told her that she was in the mood for a tuna salad and some lemonade. Clara said she would stop by the deli and pick up the bread, tuna and lettuce and that Bernice could make the lemonade if she felt like it. Clara told Bernice she would be there at about noon as usual then they hung up the phone.

Bernice was seated in the kitchen in the back of the house preparing to make the lemonade when the front door bell rang. She walked through the livingroom to the front door to answer it and when she got there she saw that it was the mailman with a small gift box with a card.

Bernice opened the door and took the box then went into the living to sit down and open it. Bernice sat the box aside to open and read the card first; because she did not expect a gift she wanted to know who sent it first. She opened the card and all it said, was thanks Aunt Bernice sorry we are late in sending this. Although the card did not have a name on it she just assumed it was from Walter and his children. Then she turned her attention to the small box and began to open it.

As she pulled at the wrapping paper and then lifted the box top off the phone in the foyer rang. She gently put the box down and went and answered the phone. It was Clara wanting to know if she should pick up anything to make the lemonade with. Bernice said no but if she would hold on for a second she would tell her what Walter had sent her. Before Clara could say a word Bernice laid the phone receiver down on the table and went to finish opening the gift box.

The DEADLY MAILMAN

Suddenly there was a loud explosion and the phone went dead. Clara became hysterical and dropped the phone and ran out to her sister's house. By the time Clara arrived she could see the fire truck pull up. There was smoke and glasses everywhere. When Clara run up on the fire chief and asked what had happened a fire team was carrying Bernice's body out and laying it on a stretcher. Clara broke down crying right there.

Jason Beckett's Law Office

At 8:00am the next morning seated in the waiting area of Jason Beckett's law office was U.S. Marshal Harry Bailey and his assistant U.S. Marshal Laura McKnight.

At 8:05am the firms receptionist team stepped off of the elevator and upon seeing the 6'4", 225 lb muscular well dressed brown skinned Marshal Bailey with badge and handgun under his short jacket and then the lovely long wavy black haired 5' 11", shapely, 185 lb Dominican American Marshal McKnight; they greeted them took their names, offered them coffee and attempted to immediately contact Attorney's Jason and or Mark, to determine what time if at all either would arrive.

At 8:10am Jason Beckett stepped off of the office elevator and introduced himself to Marshal's Bailey and McKnight. He invited them into his office while he got pulled some documents together to show them and waited for his partner City Councilmen Mark Oliver to arrive.

City Councilmen Oliver arrived at 8:30am sharp and the four begin to discuss the case. Jason reiterated the concerns he had and Mark confirmed his statements at the earlier teleconference.

Marshal Bailey told the men that he had secured some important information and would be following it up over the next few days. Afterwards he should be prepared to report back to all concerned what if he anything they had learned. Then the Marshal's left to visit with John Mason's accountant and business attorney but they had to make one stop before they did. Marshal's Bailey and McKnight had decided to stop by John Mason's office building and see if there were any building entrance or exit security video footage available.

Marshal Bailey's idea was now that they had uncovered several facial recognition matches of Fred Beckett the suspected tie between Mason and the tie between this suspected mystery man and John had to be confirmed. Marshal Bailey figured if there was an impostor and that impostor was tied to Mason there might have been a face to face meeting between the two in the days leading up to the kidnapping and checking the office building security video files was as good a place to start.

When Marshal's Bailey and Laura finished meeting with the building security officer they had several clips of a man fitting the description of the impostor coming and leaving the premises. They could not determine if there was a fitted pattern to his arrivals or departures other than most arrivals were at 10:00am sharp. That bit of information prompted Marshal Laura to contact the local precinct commander and asked for a team to stake out the building once a day for the next 10 days between the hours of 9:30am and 11:00am. He agreed.

Goldman and Ricketts CPA's and Tax Professionals

Marshal's Bailey and Laura left Mason's office

building and went directly to Goldman and Ricketts CPA's and Tax Professionals John mason and Fred Beckett's corporate accountants offices. When the Marshal's arrived they found both Ira Goldman and Clint Ricketts in the middle of shredding files. Marshal Bailey asked what they were doing and they asked why he wanted to know. Marshal Bailey quickly responded and said, "We are investigating your relationship with John mason and Fred Beckett. Are any of those documents associated with their account?" Ira Goldman breathe a sign of relief, sat down and said, "No these are someone else's files duplicate files. How can we help you?"

Marshal Bailey pull out the photo of Fred Beckett and the three other similar faces and laid them on the desk and said, "Would you be kind enough to tell which if any of these four men you have been in contact with in the last 30 days?"

Ira looked and then he looked closely, finally he asked Clint to take a look and for a moment he was hard pressed to confirm their meeting with Fred Beckett as opposed to any of the other three. Finally Ira said, "Marshal I'd love to help you but the only thing I am sure of is that Fred Beckett was one of our larger clients for a number of years up until his death a couple of weeks ago. As far as picking his face out of this array of photos I just can't be sure." Clint agreed.

The last stop Marshal's Bailey and Laura made that day was at John Mason's corporate attorney's office, again to confirm the closeness of likeness between Fred Beckett and the prospective sampling of impostors. Again Mason's own attorney could tell the difference between Fred Beckett's photo and that of any of the other three potential impostors.

As soon as Marshal Bailey left the attorney's office he called in for a wire tap on all of John Mason's phones. Then he called John Mason and scheduled a face to face meeting at Mason's office for the next day.

CHAPTER 7

THE DAY CARE CENTER

The next morning at 9:00am Lou Gallo was standing in the lobby of his New Jersey office building checking his mailbox when a mailman came up to him and asked him if he was Lou Gallo. Lou said, "And what of it?" The mailman said, "Great the doorman said I might find you over here. I have a certified letter for you. Would you please sign for it?" Lou looked at him and then he said, "How do I know you are really a mailman?" The Mailman said, "Because I am delivering you your mail!" Then Lou reached for the mailman's signature board and said, "You sure you ain't a process server?" The told the signature board back and handed Lou the letter and responded, "I'm sure" then he walked away.

Lou looked at the letter and immediately he knew who it was from and he said to himself, 'Damn a process server." The letter was from Nationwide Insurance Company's Audit department. It was a final demand notice telling him that unless he makes his files available for inspection his contract to write with them and any of its affiliates would be terminated immediately and subject to a state ethnics and fraud review.

Lou hadn't had any experience in this area but he knew it didn't sound good so Lou walked over to the news stand and picked up the days newspaper and then went upstairs to his office to call and make an appointment for re-insurance companies auditors to stop by that coming Monday at 10:00am.

After the call Lou opened his newspaper and saw the half page photo and article about the fire bomb incident at elderly Ms. Bernice's home in Brooklyn and he called John Mason's office.

Lou tells John to pick up a copy of the day's Daily News and check out page 6 and that he will be by around noon to see him. John responded and said, After 4:00pm would be better, he was waiting on a call about getting some additional funding. Lou said, "So your partners came through?" John responded and said, "I'll let you know" then he hung up.

Lou immediately called Eddie Rocco to confirm the afternoon meeting. Eddie told Lou to sit tight, but he didn't confirm whether he or Joey had a meeting planned for that afternoon with John. A few minutes latter Eddie called Lou back and said, "It looks like there are more teams on the playing field then we initially thought. So it looks like we are going to play along until it's our turn up at bat. And oh! By the way, you've been moved up to the coaching box. First thing tomorrow stop by there and check the books, get the vig and drop it at the usual spot. The vig will be $50 large. Take $10 off the top for yourself. You know the drop spot." And then he hung up.

Marshal Bailey and Marshal Laura arrive at John Mason's office

John mason's secretary showed Marshal's Bailey and Laura in to John's office at around 1:00pm that afternoon. After some chit chat Marshal Bailey asked John if he thought there was any truth to his former business partner's son claim that some kidnapped his father and had an impersonator forge his signature on various legal documents. John went on and on about Jason's imaginary impostor and his mean spiritedness against him and his business acumen.

Marshal Bailey then showed John the photo array and asked him if he could recognize Fred Beckett's picture among the group. John hesitated for a minute and then he picked Fred's picture out. Then Marshal Bailey if John knew any of the other people in the array and John trying to look surprised said, "I thought they were all of Fred." Marshal Bailey said, "So why did you pick that particular photo?" John shrugged his shoulders and said, "It was the best likeness of him I thought."

As Marshal Bailey and Laura got up to leave, Marshal Bailey asked john were he was the night Fred Beckett was killed. John said, "I was at home, alone, why?"

Marshal Bailey responded and said, "Routine, that is all. Just routine." Then they left the office and walked out into the elevator lobby and as they got unto an elevator they saw Eddie Rocco and his Cousin Joey with his arm in a sing, and four 250 to 300 lb body guards, get off carrying two large suit cases. Marshal Bailey commented to Marshal Laura, "Did you see that?" Marshal Laura responded and said, "Eddie 'Pots and Pans' Rocco and his cousin 'Two thumbs' Joey, I believe." Then Marshal Bailey said, I think we just I.D. our suspect now all we have to do make the case."

Marshal Laura said, "What was with the photo

The DEADLY MAILMAN

I.D.? I mean how could he immediately recognize Fred Beckett when his own son couldn't tell the faces apart." Marshal Bailey smiled and said, "Because he knew which one wasn't Beckett." Then Marshal Bailey said, let's go over to John Mason's home in Great Neck Long Island, and see if there are any surveillance camera's in the area that might confirm or dispel his alibi. And they left.

Back inside John Mason's office when Eddie and Joey walked in to the office while the body guards waited right outside. John was on the phone with the Lucci Brothers about to make arrangements to come by and pick up the loan. He put them on hold and as soon as he realized that the Rocco brothers were ready to make a deal he brushed the Lucci brothers off until another opportunity arose. Eddie and Joey heard enough of the conversation to figure out what had just happened, they just didn't know exactly who John was talking too, so they acted like they weren't interested in what was being said.

When John hung up the phone Eddie said, "John first things first, you should apologize to Joey here for shooting him in the arm. He is in a lot of pain and it was your bullheadedness that caused it. Now I talked to Joey and explained sometimes business deals get a little heated and he is willing to forgive you if you do the right thing and apologize."

John looked at Joey and started to say something other than 'I apologize' and Eddie interrupted him and said, "And John be sincere" then he pulled out his handgun and laid it on his lap. John knew he was out played and that they had nothing to lose so he rethought his attitude and made a sincere apologize the best way he could. Joey thought about it for a minute and Eddie lifted up his gun from his lap and when Joey saw that he said, "No Eddie, I understand it is ok. I accept his apology." Eddie put his gun back in his waistband and said, "We got your money here. And we agree to all of the terms. Any questions?"

John stood up and walked around the desk to look in the suitcases. He lifted each one up and sat it on the desk, then opened them and sorted through the bungled stacks. He then walked over to his wall safe and opened it and started to stack it in, row after row after row. Eddie looked at the safe and said, "You got enough room in there?" John said, "It was built to hold $5 million. It's actually very deceiving.' When John finished the suitcases were empty and the safe still looked like there was room in it. Both Eddie and Joey shook john's hand and as they turned to walk out Eddie said, "There is going to be a price to pay for Mr. Rosenberg you know that. I'll let you choose the payment date. You got 30 days to give us a date. We'll tell you what the cost will be." Then the two walked out and closed the door.

At 3:00pm John left his office and took a limo over to Widow Mosby's Laundromat

When John arrived at Clara Mosby's Laundromat he wasn't surprised when he didn't see her at her usual station so he had his driver take him to Clara's sister Bernice's place which was just down the street.

When he pulled up Clara was standing outside talking to a contractor and the funeral director.

John gets out of the limo and rest on the rear trunk of the car while Clara continues her conversation with the Funeral Director. At this point her plans for burying her sister were on hold while the Fire Marshal and the Bomb Square investigated the cause of the explosion. John could see that Clara was very distraught and when she turned her attention to him he proceeded with caution as he spoke.

The DEADLY MAILMAN

John said, "I just read in the paper about the terrible accident and thought I should come by and extend my condolences. I am sorry for your loss I know you and your sister were very close." Then he turned to get into his car.

Clara paused for a moment and said, "I have been very mean to you and you have always been so nice. So please accept my apologize for my behavior. And thanks for stopping by." Then she paused and as John began to close the car door behind him she knocked on the window and waved him to roll it down. He did and she said, "You know now that my sister is gone I really don't have anyone here to nurse, if you can up your offer to $850,000, all cash I'm ready to sign."

John smiled and said, "The best I can do all cash right now is $800,000 I can have my attorney stop by later today with the acceptance agreement and quick claim and you can stop by the bank tomorrow morning and bring your suitcase for the cash." Clara reached in the window and said, "Well $800,000 will be acceptable for the building alone; the equipment and the business are separate. I think I'll cut a deal with my part timers to see if they want to take it over or just buy the equipment. But if you want the building vacant I'll need to get a broker to sell my equipment outright. I've been thinking about retiring to Florida with my son and his wife for a while so this should work out fine. Looks like we have a deal Mr. Mason, thanks and see you in the morning."

U.S. Marshal's Regional Office Federal Plaza Downtown Manhattan

Marshal Bailey was seated at his desk talking to Marshal Laura when Supervising Marshal Bert Cooke walked in and asked for an update on the Beckett Case.

Harry responded and said, "The first bit of good news was the receipt of the facial recognition prospects. This guy Beckett's face wasn't that unusual after all. We got three hits but the closes one in looks and location was a Lou Gallo here in the metro area. Of the three people we asked to verify that this guy could be the impostor only one identified the victim without hesitation, that was our main suspect John Mason.

Then we got security video from Mason's office building around the time of the murder that captured this guy Gallo visiting on a weekly basis.

T&e DEADLY MAILMAN

When we pressed Mason for an alibi for the night of the murder he said he was home alone but again security footage from his gated community security booth shows he left his home with a sufficient amount of time to commit the murder and be at the scene during the initial interview.

Right now we have Mason's office building under surveillance in an effort to spot this Lou Gallo again and find out where he is staying so we can get a search warrant when we pick him up and bring him in for questioning." Bert interrupted and said, "Lou Gallo! What do we know about him, anything?"

Harry pulled open a folder on his desk and started to read. He said, Lou Gallo had a 8 page long rap sheet with almost 100 felony type charges but no convictions. Over his short 50 year life span he has been accused of assault, assault with a deadly weapon, intent, intent with a deadly weapon, loan sharking, racketeering, intent to racketeer, witness tampering, intent and a host of other unsavory charges. None of which resulted in any convictions. The footnote say's he is armed and extremely dangerous yet no convictions. All this tells us is no one has ever pent a body to him. He's got no family, never been married and no child support obligations. He has several residences and several business addresses listed in his file but none showing any recent visits for verification purposes. The guy is like a ghost. No bank accounts in his name, at least in this country. And what's funny, no interrogations I the last 5 years. Could this guy have gone straight?

Harry looked up at Bert and Laura and they all laughed and said, "Na that can't be right."

Harry continued and said, "And by the way, we are waiting to hear from my brother at the bureau to see what ties this Mason guy may have to the Rocco Family we saw them making a visit to Mason's office earlier today. And get this they were carrying two large suitcases and followed by four armed guards."

Bert said, "I knew you'd be all over it, you are my best team." Harry said, Boss you say that about all of your teams, when they are in the flow." Bert smiled and said, "Yes I do, because that is when it is true." Everyone laughed out loud and then Bert said, "Now for the reality check. Your brother Ralph called and said, "Back for of the Rocco Family they got to many hours in on them and your guy Mason maybe a new player and an unexpected to key to their take down. Now I don't know why he didn't call you first but, that is what he told me. I guess he didn't want to be the one to blow your case out of the water? So after you two work that out call me and let me know the plan. Goodnight."

As soon as Bert walked out Harry looked at Laura and said, "It's a good thing my brothers office in only a few flights away, let's go upstairs and visit him and find out first hand what he is talking about.

John Mason's Office 4:00pm that afternoon

John is seated at his desk when Lou walked in and said, "Hello, I'm here." John said, "I thought you were going to call, ahead?" Lou smiled and said, "To much to do, so I thought I save myself some time and just come right over. You got my money?" John got up and walked over to the safe and opened it. He counted out $25 large and handed it to Lou. Then he said, "Nice work on the widows sister I met with her this morning and she came around and accepted the offer. It closed at a little more than I expected but by this time tomorrow I'll be down to the last two properties and we're running out of time."

The DEADLY MAILMAN

Lou said, "I'm a man of my word, where is the next place?" John sat back down behind his desk and said, "You know where the auto repair shop was? And the widows spot? This last one is a large day care behind the widows spot but adjacent to the auto spot. The address is on 7th Ave. It is called the Little Hero's Day Care. The owner is a Karen Allen. She lives upstairs to the place as well. I offered her $700 large last year and she kicked me out. I guess she knew what the property was worth, at that time just over a mil. Right now I guess it's worth $1.25 mil easy. I want it for $800 large, not a penny more."

Lou smiled and said, "I'll take care of it before Tuesday, does that work for you?" John responded and said, "Good, Mark will be retiring at the end of the week. But be careful, it's only her and her teenage son there. If you take her out then it will fall to her son who can't make a decision the courts will appoint a guardian and that could take forever to work in my favor. Focus on the son, make her a widow maybe she'll want to sell and move south like the other one."

Then John stood up as if to walk Lou to the door and Lou said, "What's going on? You in a rush?" John said, "Not really but you are so businesslike, in and out within two or three minutes I figured you were ready to go. Was there something else?"

Lou said, "Have a seat there is one more thing we need to go over. You got a drink?"

John said, "Oh! I didn't know you indulged. What would you like?" Lou said, "Give me a class of the cognac over there." John said, "Ice?"

Lou said, "No neat is best." John grabbed a couple of classes and sat the bottle on the desk in front of Lou and then he sat down behind his desk and poured a class for himself.

As Lou fiddled with the bottle cork and eventually poured himself a stiff drink he said, "John! I see you and the Rocco brothers are on good business terms. I heard about the little accident the other day; you the one where Mr. Rosenberg was permanently retired?" John sat up and said, "Oh! You heard about that? From who?"

Lou sat the bottle back on the desk, but held onto the cork as he responded and said, "From my new employers. I have been asked to act as the monitor or go between, between you and the Rocco brothers. It seems brother Joey gets upset when he sees you still breathing after shooting him the shoulder."

John got up and walked over to the window bank, which had just been repaired, and said, "That fat bastard I would have killed him if I thought there was any other way to get out of there alive and still get that loan."

Lou said, "Not to worry, Eddie is keeping him under control, for now. If this big deal you sold them on doesn't come to light then all bets are off. You didn't hear that from me though. My job is simple. I stop by once a week, check the books, pick up the vig and life is good."

John turned around and looked at Lou then as he walked over to the wall safe again he said, "So you here to pick up the vig? What is it this time?"

John begins to open the safe. Lou takes out two small vials. One he empties into the bottle of cognac and the other he dips onto the bottom of the cork. Then he places the cork back into the bottle and stands up and places it back in the bar rack behind John's desk. John turned and saw Lou place the bottle back on the rack and said, "So how much is it this week?"

Lou turned and looked at him and said, "This week! It's $50 large. What were the collections for this week?"

John started to ignore Lou's question and just handed him the money. Lou took the money and said, "Now I'm not going to ask you again. I'll just send Joey's two sons back over here and let them finish the job they started the last time they were here. I assume this time they'll just walk you up to the fifth floor and dump your ass off the roof."

John signed and said, "The collections are the same every week, $125 large. That is just enough to cover the overhead until these recent purchases can be converted and brought online. How many times do I have to tell you people that?"

Lou smiled and said, "You people! You people? You say that as if to insult us. I tell you this; you people are the reason why people like us exist. If it wasn't for you people none of this would be necessary. So when I tell you it never pleases me to take a life. I'll make an exception if comes to you people." Then he walked to the door and as he opened it he said, "I'll see you next week, same time." Then he left.

John's cellphone rings as the door closes behind Lou, its Vince. He asked John if he felt like a little excitement later on that night. John said, "Are we talking about more of the same?" Vince said, "No I'm thinking we need to change it up a little bit, this time all bets are in on the second round. I'm gonna feel a little sleepy by then." John laughed and said, "Isn't it my job to call for naps?" Vince said, "This is leisure income and the only way to guarantee it is to play it close to the vest. Besides I'm not as young as I used to be. Recuperation takes a lot longer now then it used to, so I have to manage my beatings."

John said, "Of course, same place same time." Vince said, "See you then" and he hung up.

Marshal's Bailey and Laura arrive at Special Agent Ralph Bailey's Office on the 26th Floor of Federal Plaza

When Marshal's Bailey and Laura walked into Agent Ralph's office his secretary greeted them and watched them walk right in. Ralph was eating lunch at his desk and just gazed at the two when they walked in and sat down in front of his desk.

Finishing his bite he said, "Hello Marshal Laura how are you this fine morning? You are looking as beautiful as ever, as usual." Harry sat quietly and waited for Ralph to finish then he said, "You don't have to speak to me, but when I tell your mother how you've treating me, watch out." Both men and Laura laughed out loud for a moment. Then Ralph said, "So what took you so long? Was the elevator out of service between the 12 and the 26th floor?"

Harry smiled and said, "No more out of service then it was when you told my boss that you had first dibs on my chief suspect."

Ralph said, "Little brother I know you've been in this business for what 10 years maybe 15 if we count the early military days, but this is the big league here on the 26th floor we put people away permanently if you need me to spell it out for you."

Harry looked at Laura and said, "Oh! No he didn't go there, did he?"

Laura smiled and said, "You two are worst then teenager with this sometimes. Now Ralph you know we need this guy Mason on this identity theft scheme and who knows what else we are going to find now that our case is coming together. Besides you can give him to us and then leverage our case to get him to rollover on his other friends, the Rocco's."

Harry looked at Laura and said, "Good argument, but those were my facts."

Ralph said, "Yea, but since she said, it I can better understand the point. And maybe go along with it. I'll have to see how this whole thing pans out."

Then Harry said, "Look Ralph can we be serious for a minute? This guy John Mason how long has he been on your radar? And what kind of player is he?"

Ralph said, "We have picked up a few conversations between him and the brothers but he wasn't really a player until just this week. He killed their council of 30 years in a fit of rage. We are still following that. He got them to loan him $3 million dollars cash; while playing the Rocco boys against the Lucci brothers. The Rocco's just delivered the cash to him the other day. He is in the middle of some kind of parking lot empire expansion focused on the Barclay's Sports Center deal. We know he has at least one City Councilmen in his pocket. Right now we are trying to pull this whole thing with him together to see how valuable an asset he might be. And you want him on a identity theft rap? What can he get for that? Five to ten maybe? I got him on murder 2 and loan sharking without breaking a sweat. Why would I give him to you?"

Harry said, "Well he may committed a murder 1 act in the midst of the identity theft and we can make him on the loan sharking with your help as well. Give us a week and then let's see who has the stringer case. Laura makes some good points. You can always give him to us and then leverage our case to get him to roll on his friends the Rocco's. Now what can you tell me about Lou Gallo?"

Ralph reached in his desk drawer and pulled out a file about an inch thick and said, "Lou Gallo is a made man in the Rocco Family. He has worked for the family for over 30 years. A one time collector, loan shark and now freelance hitman Lou Gallo is the kind of person who could blend in at a family bar-be-que or beach party and cut your throat in the cabana be cocktails. Gallo is as cold a killer as there comes. Extensive rap sheet, I'm sure you know but no convictions because he always knows when to move on. Just when the heat gets close he disappears."

Harry said, "So where can we find him?"

Ralph responded and said, "Don't know we are

interested in him right now. He seems to be flowing around in ear shot but up until yesterday wasn't a player in our case. Yesterday he was given matching orders to be the watchdog between the Rocco brothers and John Mason. He is now the main go between the family and Mason to collect and watch the books for them. That way the younger brother Joey won't have to see Mason and be reminded of his shooting him in the shoulder. I guess it will keep Mason alive long enough for these guys to make some money and then they will have Gallo eliminate him."

As Ralph continued a phone call came in. It was one of his field agents with an update on the Rocco brothers. When Ralph finished talking he got up to leave and Harry asked him where he could find Lou Gallo. Ralph said, "He just left Mason's office." Harry asked if Ralph's people got a plate number or something they could use to find him and Ralph said, "No, he's not the priority here but we'll keep you in mind over the next week or so." Then they all left the office.

Downtown Fight Club 3:00am

Vince and John walked into the fight club to a standing ovation. When Rickie heard what had happened he personally walked down and to the ring level and asked john to join him in the promoters room, so he didn't have to wait until Vince fought to relax and beat. John followed him upstairs to the mezzanine and joined in the frenzy.

Ricky told John Vince was going to fight last tonight because he felt the money would be running high for his return to the ring. Besides Ricky had a special opponent in the wings and he expected some heavy betters to arrive by then.

As planned John was ready to bet upwards of $50 large on Vince to win the first round and then up to $100 large on his losing the second round by knock out.

The plan worked like a charm right up to the last minute of the first round when Vince was elbowed so hard to the back of the head that only the bell saved him from a knock out. Then John was confused as to what to do. Vince did not tell him that he would have any real or contrived difficulty winning the first round but he lost. John had expected to parlay his winnings from the first round into the second round and with the lost he was at a disadvantage. Now he has to decide for himself what to do.

The DEADLY MAILMAN

The hostess came over and asked john what was going to be his pleasure in the second round and john said, "$50 large on the opponent to win." The hostess smiled and said, "Recovery is a good thing" and she walked away.

When the bell rang for the start of the second round, the crowd was riled up with expectation. Vince had a history, although brief of coming from behind but after the wiping he took in the first round no one was sure what to expect.

The bell rang and Vince came out swinging and kicking. The man is on fire john heard someone say. And he could see the fire in Vince's eyes from the first round house kick to the left handed upper cut. Vince put up the fight of his life during that 3 minute round but it wasn't enough. In the end his opponent took him down with what he called was the Queen hand salute. He grabbed Vince's right forearm with his left hand, pulled him to him and straddled it with his right leg and kicked Vince under the chin three times with it, knocking him out cold as a fish. The crowd went wild. John broke even and tipped Vince $10 large for his showing. After the battle the two went out to breakfast at a nearby diner eventhough was pretty well beat up.

The DEADLY MAILMAN

Once the two sat down and ordered John asked Vince what happened. Vince said, "I heard that my opponent was Ricky favorite from out of town. Brought in especially to fight me. You see eventhough I maybe new around here I'm not new to this game, I just pick and chose my battles very carefully. I've seen that guy before and I know I can beat him. That queen hand salute move my brother taught him and I taught it to my brother, so you know I know how to defend against it. But I had to take the ass wiping tonight believe me, it was better than what they had planned if he had lost.

John looked confused and said, "You mean these fights are fixed?" Vince smiled and sipped his coffee and didn't say a word. Then John said, "So you fix fixed fights? How does that work?"

Vince said, "It's all in the game my friend. It's all in the game. This week you win, next week I win. What are you gonna do. That's what makes the world go round."

John said, "That might be how your world goes but mine doesn't. I wasted my time to night, I needed to make some money and now I'm 410 large in the whole. So what's the plan?"

The DEADLY MAILMAN

Vince signed and said, "This is the business I'm in, you win some, you lose some. I'll be back in two weeks and we'll get your money back plus some, not a problem." John said, "Look how would you like to make a few dollars in the mean time a little easy work?"

Vince said, "How much?" John said, "10 large for one minutes work." Vince said, "As long as that minute doesn't cost me a life time I'm listening." John said, "My partner hired this guy to do some dirty work for us and now his has gotten out of control. He does things with out our consent and then he wants to be paid for it. He's a lose canon I tell you. I just need him taken care of; permanently you know what I mean."

John continued and said, "His name is Lou, Lou Gallo. You don't have to worry about anything I'll set the whole thing up. You got a peace?" Vince said, "No guns. I'll take care of it, trust me."

John said, "Ok, I'll call you around Wednesday evening. No, no Thursday evening when he comes by my office around 4:00pm you can catch him in the parking garage in my office building, make it look like a robbery, he'll have cash on him. That will work." Vince said, "No problem, call me."

Friday morning 11:00am Rocco's Trucking and Moving Service

Patti showed up for work late as usual but this time she arrived at 11:00am verses her usual 10:00am strut in. Eddie was seated at his desk counting last nights gambling take and Joey was eating a hero sandwich for breakfast.

Eddie watched Patti stroll in and over to her desk until he couldn't stand it anymore and he said, "Patti, you think this is your business? Who the Hell are you to come strolling in here late and not say a word? Where you been? Something important could have happened and God forbid we needed you and you stroll in here at what? 11:00am! What's going on here?"

Patti settled in and said, "Did anything happen while I was gone?"

Eddie yelled back, "Thank God no."

Patti said, "Good so what you crying about? I always come in at this time when I'm out gathering information that is important to your loan business."

Now Eddie's curiosity is peaked and he calmed

down and said, "Gathering information about our loan business? And what information could that be, Patti?"

Patti turned her chair to the wall and said, "I'm not telling you until you be nice to me. You know I have to get my kids off to the baby sitter in the morning and today I was late because of the information I got for you last night. So stop being mean to me or I won't tell you."

Eddie reached in his desk drawer and pulled out a barber's razor and laid it on the desk and said, "Tell me what?"

Patti turned around just in time to see Eddie lay the razor down on the desk and then she perked up and said, "No need to get mad, I'll tell you. I saw that guy Mason at the fight club last night and he was betting heavy on some washed up fighter named Vince. And John lost big time, almost $100 large I guess."

Eddie turned to Joey and said, "This guy is promoting with our money? And losing?"

Joey puts his sandwich down and said to Patti, "Vince who?"

Patti said, "Vince, Vince Carbone you know

Hard Head Vince Carbone."

Eddie looked at Joey and then Joey and Eddie got up and walked out into the warehouse behind a couple of trucks to talk. Joey said, "This guy Mason has lost his mind. Does he think he can get Hard Head Carbone to whack one of us? I told you we should have whacked him when he shot Rosenberg, now he's out of control."

Eddie said, "Calm down you are the only one out of control here, right now." The two men thought for a few minutes and finally Eddie said, "Look this what we are going to do. This guy Mason will be finished signing up all of those properties he's been crying about in a few days. He's using Lou to pull it off, so the day Lou finds out where the last property is, we have him take out Hard Head and then we have Lou get rid of Mason. That why we have all of the properties and no partners." Joey smiled and said, "So we'll be the parking lot kings of New York, right? But whose gonna run them?" Eddie said, "We'll have Lou run them, he'll know the business by then. I mean how hard could it be? Open the lot, collect the money, close the lot. Like making pizza, both men laughed out loud and then went back inside the office. When had resumed their activities Eddie said to Joey, "Call Lou and tell him to let our friend Mason know that we have figure out what restitution we want, but don't tell what it is. Just let him know it ain't him and it will be over before he knows it. And leave it at that, he'll call if he wants more details. Which we won't give him." The men laughed again.

Independent Security Corporation, Great Neck Long Island, NY

Seated in the office of Independent Security Corporation Vice President of Marketing Phillip Elliot were Marshal's Bailey and Laura waiting for Mr. Elliot to return with footage of the main gate at John Mason's cul-da-sac the night of Fred Beckett's murder.

Harry had asked if the company could provide both a sample copy and a certified copy for evidence purposes. When Mr. Elliot returned he thanked Harry and Laura for being curious enough to not leak to the press that one of their clients was under investigation ad that the company was cooperating and then they left.

By the time Harry and Laura had arrived at County Police Headquarters in Mineola Great Neck Police Chief Raymond Hoyt was sitting in Detective Captain Bullock's office waiting for their arrival. Captain Bullock introduced Police Chief Hoyt to Marshal's Bailey and Laura as everyone took seats for an unscheduled update into the investigation from the Marshal's.

Harry spoke first and said, "Chief Hoyt what brings you here?" Chief Hoyt smiled and said, "I wasn't sure why you guy's were looking into the whereabouts of John Mason so I thought I'd stop in see if I could lean a hand. Mason is a longtime resident of the Great Neck community and he is well respected. So if there is a need for someone to vouch for the man's character, let me be included on that list."

Harry shook his head and said, "Why thank you chief for taking the time to stop by and offer your support. By the way how did you know we were looking into Mr. Mason's whereabouts?" Chief Hoyt turned red in the face and said, "I'm sorry I thought I said, we live in a small community and that john Mason was one of our most respected members."

Harry shook his head again and then looked around the room. When his eyes returned to the Chief he said, "So John Mason is a pillar in the community? Is he one of the elected official's there?"

Chief Hoyt said, "Why yes he is! He is one of the oldest Village Trustees. Elections are scheduled for next month matter a fact."

Harry shook his head again and then said, "Well thank you Chief Hoyt for stopping by and if we find any reason to question Mr. Mason's character we will certainly let you know. Thanks again."

81st and 3rd Avenue All Day Parking Lot

Before John could get out of his limo to collect the weeks receipts a crush of news reporters surrounded it. He could see the Police forensic team van parked in the rear of the lot and several police cars blocking off the street. John pushed his way through the crowd of reporters and lookie lou's to the Lot Managers booth. Once inside he saw his guy Lewis talking to 2 NYPD Detectives. Lewis introduced John as the lot owner and said, "Boss I don't know what happened, a customer complained about the smell coming from one of the cars by the time I got over to check it out the cops, the news, the everybody was already in the lot. Sorry I didn't have a second to call you."

John turned to one of the detectives and said, "My name is John Mason I'm the owner, what's going on?"

The detective said, "My name is Det. Jessie Longstreet and this is my partner Det. Alex Riveria, we are from the 46th precinct Midtown it looks like you have a dead body in the trunk of a high end vehicle, do you know anything about it?"

John looked at him and said, "What are you a comedian? I just got here. How could I know anything about it?"

Det. Longstreet smiled and said, "Was that a corporate limo you drove up in?"

John said, "Yea! What about it? We have several at our disposal."

Det. Riveria said, "So where is your car?"

John said, "I lent it to a friend, why?"

Det. Longstreet said, "When was that?"

John said, "A couple of days ago why?"

Det. Riveria said, "Why would your friend need to borrow your car for a couple of days? Why didn't you just give him access to one of your corporate limo's?"

John said, "He liked the color I don't know. It wasn't a big deal. What is going on here? Why aren't you answering my question?"

Det. Longstreet said, "I've got some answers for you but I think its best we go downtown and discuss them privately, what do you say?"

John snapped back and said, "I say screw you until you answer my question what is going on here?"

Det. Riveria said, "What is this friend's name you lent your car to? And where can we find him, now?"

John walked out of the booth and over to where he saw the forensic van parked in the rear of the lot. As he approached he realized that the car the detectives were talking about was his Mercedes. He walked up on it and he could still smell the stench of death in the open trunk. He almost lost his lunch right there. Det. Longstreet caught up to him and said, "Any reason why your friend would leave a dead body in the back of your trunk?"

The DEADLY MAILMAN

John started to think quickly and he said, "I'm not sure if my friend when my friend dropped the car off, now that I think about it."

Det. Riveria said, "Oh! So now we have selected memory right? I suppose you didn't know the victim either?"

John said, "Did you see me view a body while you two were practicing your Mutt and Jeff routine back in the Lot booth? No I don't know whose body was in the trunk."

Det. Longstreet said, "Well we do, it was a friend of the Rocco Brothers Crime family their long time attorney Mr. Rosenberg. Now do you know who we are talking about?"

John said, "Rosenberg, Rosenberg an attorney, for the Rocco brothers; a crime family? No; that name doesn't ring a bell. Why do you ask?"

Det. Longstreet said, "I'll tell you why I ask, as soon as we get downtown. Now we can do this the easy way or the hard way it's your choice."

Monday morning 10:00am Lou Gallo's New Jersey Office

Stanley Morrow Assistant Audit Supervisor for the New York Region of Nationwide Insurance showed up at Lou's insurance office at 10:00am sharp and was eager to sit and go through Lou's files and books. Lou had another plan. When Stanley walked in and sat down Lou asked him to tell him about the process and what kinds of outcomes were possible.

Stanley told Lou that he had been conducting agent policy and business operation audits for over 20 years and believed that if there were any irregularities he would be the one to find them. As far as possible outcomes Stanley joke and said, "Only one person I know of has gone to jail for falsifying his books so anything is possible."

Lou smiled and said, "That was what I was afraid of." Stanley looked somewhat confused and then asked, what did he mean by that.

Lou reached in his desk as Stanley pulled out his laptop and asked if Lou had Wi-Fi; and pulled out a manila envelope and pushed it across the desk in front of Stanley.

Innocently Stanley picked it up and said, "So what is this?"

Lou said, "Open it." Stanley laid it back down and said, "Look sir I don't now what you think is going to happen here but bribery isn't going to make things any better."

Lou repeated himself and then sat back and opened his suit jacket to show the >38 s&w he had under it.

Nervously Stanley reached for the envelope, picked it up and opened it. Inside were several 8 ½" by 11" black and white photo's of Stanley walking his two 5 and 6 year old daughters to their bus stop Friday morning. In shock Stanley said, "Where did you get these?" Lou said, "A friend of mine hand delivered them to me just this morning. I thought they might come in handy during your audit. You know, give you something to focus on. You know fear and concern over a child's everyday activities is the number one issue for young parents. I mean anything could happen now-a-days."

Stanley stood up and said, "I don't want anything to happen to my girls so if it pleases you, this audit is over and you will receive a letter informing you of your satisfactory examination within the week."

Lou stood up and retrieved the envelope with the photos in it and nodded his head goodbye to Stanley as he put away his laptop and left the office.

Tuesday Morning at Little Hero's Day Care

Dressed in his Mailman uniform with a red, white and blue bandana wrapped around his neck and a white due rag under his official mailman cap, and standing behind several large cardboard boxes on his hand truck Lou rang the day centers door bell, several times fast. Checking the doors security camera first the owner a Ms. Karen Allen came and opened the door.

Lou hurriedly pushed the hand truck full of boxes just inside the doorway and handed Mr. Allen a pen and a clipboard with a blank signature on it.

As Ms. Allen pondered what was in the boxes she began twirling the pen in her hand. Lou looked at her while she looked at the boxes and said, "Look lady you gonna sign this week or not?"

Ms. Allen looked at the boxes and said, "Are you sure these are for me. I'm really not expecting anything this week. Can I take a look before I sign?"

Lou said, "Sure, look all you want, I got all day, lady."

Ms. Allen lifted the top two boxes off and did not see a label or any signage on them then when she went to lift the third box off or the fourth and last box on the hand truck she realized that the first boxes were very light and the third box seemed empty. She placed the third box on top of the other two and went to lift the fourth box she grabbed her back and said, "The first three were light as a fetter what is in this one, bricks?"

Lou smiled, closed the front door behind him and said, "No that one has a bomb in it."

Ms. Allen jumped by kept her composure and said, "Now that's not funny."

Lou grinned and said, "I'm not joking. It's a bomb made of gasoline, rat poison, nails and dynamic. It has a sophisticated detonator on it. It operates by a signal from my watch. Want to see how it works?"

Ms. Allen quickly recoiled and said, "No, no, please no. Why are you doing this? What do you want?"

Lou said, "Glad you asked. On that clipboard I

gave you is a quick claim land and building sale form. It has already been filled out and notarized. All you have to do is sign it and initial where necessary. Then email a photo of it to my lawyer's office and the County Clerk and within two hours you will have a certified check deposited into your personal account in the amount of $800,000. Then you will have between six months to a year before you have to vacate the premises. Or I'll detonate the bomb."

Ms. Allen said, "You are going to detonate the bomb while you are standing there?"

Lou said, "Oh know, you see I can get out before the bomb goes off, you can get out before the bomb goes off and between you and your assistant maybe you can save two or four of the 10 kids here. The question is whether it is easier for you to live with explaining to the parents of the other five or six kids why their child wasn't saved. Or on the other hand, you can just sign over the property and take the cash, keep on operating and then just go away with your life. Which will it be?"

Ms. Allen looked at her assistant and the around at the little four and five year olds in her care and said, "The property is worth over a million dollars and then my business income. Why are you doing this to me? Aren't there other properties, in better locations?"

Lou said, "Tick, tock, tick... You got less than one minute to decide. It really doesn't matter to me one way or the other. I'll blow this up today, come back kill you and blow up the new owner, I still get paid. Tick, tock, tick..."

Ms. Allen began to cry and sign the quick claim form.

CHAPTER 8

OLD MAN HARPER'S PLACE

Next day at Stanley Morrow Office, Midtown Manhattan

It was 10:30am and Stanley had just gotten off the phone with his secretary who told him that his supervisor Phillip Westing had asked to see him as soon as possible.

Stanley didn't know exactly what Mr. Westing wanted but he knew it would be important if he said as soon as possible. So he quickly gathered up his weekly audit review summary sheets and went upstairs to Mr. Westing's office.

As soon as Stanley walked into Mr. Westing's office he could feel the stress. He announced himself to one of Mr. Westing's three secretaries and she immediately ushered him past the line of waiting executives into Mr. Westing's private suite and directed him to wait in his outer office lobby. She told him Mr. Westing wanting to see him immediately.

The DEADLY MAILMAN

In Stanley's two years in the Westing's audit division he had never been in Mr. Westing's private suite so this summons had to be very important.

After about 15 minutes Mr. Westing's private secretary stepped out of the office and asked Stanley to come in. Westing was on the phone to the Washington D.C. office and he was making it clear that he was about to address the matter at hand with all deliberation and then he hung up the phone as the secretary left the room.

Westing looked up at Stanley and asked him if he knew why he was called to his office. Stanley sheepishly said, "No Sir. But I assume it is about one of my audits." Westing looked at Stanley and said, "Good you're not as dumb as you made me out to be." Stanley looking confused didn't say a word.

Then Westing said, "Your audits are consistently among the best, the most thorough, the timeliest and the most accurate around here. So when your report came in on a Mr. Sam Gold's agency in New Jersey I was shocked that you'd failed to check his bank accounts before you wrote that you considered his operation satisfactory. Did you even bother to look at his bank records?"

Stanley just looked at him and put his head down.

Mr. Westing signed and said, "Not to worry Stan. It happens to everyone sooner or later. The question is how you handle it is whether you survive around here or not. So tell me what happened."

Stanley explained what transpired at Sam's office earlier that week and begged for forgiveness. Mr. Westing was silent then he said, "I want you to go home and get your family. We have a corporate condo herein midtown you and your family can stay there until we resolve this issue. Don't worry about a thing. You don't even need to pack a bag just get them and bring them back here, my secretary will walk you through everything else; from toothbrushes to homework we got this. And just so you know, we pulled all of Gold's bank records from each of the re-insurers he did business with. For the last two years he has deposited close to $5 million dollars in policyholder death benefits checks in 9 different business accounts and funneled every dollar back to him in one way or another. By using bogus business accounts and fake names

The DEADLY MAILMAN

we believe he has managed to swindle each of his re-insurers out of more than $10 million dollars. Right now we aren't even sure the dead benefits paid out were even for policies written to people who were alive when the actual policy was taken out. I mean some of this could be blamed on the re-insurer for one reason or another but in the final analysis this Sam Gold has played more games out of that one small office then all of the suspected fraudulent policy writers I seen in my 30 year history here at Nationwide. I guess when he was confronted with you it didn't really matter one way or the other. He is probably planning of leaving the country as we speak if he hasn't already. But we'll get him. I have a call into a friend of mine at the FBI right now. We'll get him and anyone else who maybe involved. Don't you worry. Now go home and get your family. Don't even call them, just go get them and bring them here. Go."

Mr. Westing continued and said, "As Stanley got up to walk out of the office door, "This guy Sam Gold might be an old con artist but he's not too old to go to jail, for final few years of his thieving life." Stanley turned around and said, "He's not that old he probably has another 40 years on him easy."

Westing said, "Wait! What are you talking about this guy Sam Gold is easily 81 or 82 years old if he makes another 4 or 5 years he'll be lucky."

Stanley stopped dead in his tracks and said, "No boss Sam Gold is at best 40 years old and at worst 45 my 50 not a day older."

Westing reached over and pulled Sam Gold's file back in front of him and pulled out his license photo and showed it to Stanley and said, "This guy looks 40 to 50 years old to you?"

Stanley looked with shock and said, "That's not Sam Gold." Westing looked at him and said, "Trust me that is old Sam Gold I've seen him enough times at luncheons and other meetings of the last 30 years to know him when I see him." Stanley said, "Well the man I met with was 40 years old, short kind of stocky, dark hair, round face, looked Italy."

Westing said, "You go get your family and then you are going to have to go to downtown to the Fed's office and work with a sketch artist so we can figure this one out."

46th Precinct Interrogation Room 1

T&e DEADLY MAILMAN

Seated in front of John Mason at the small steel gray table in the interrogation room was Det. Longstreet and standing behind John was Det. Riveria.

Det. Riveria hounded John as to why he wanted Mr. Rosenberg dead while Det. Longstreet picked away at John's alibi of being alone in his office at the time of the incident; when Attorney Robert Conner's was escorted in by another police officer.

Det. Riveria asked the officer who was the guest and he responded and said, "This is Attorney Robert Conner's Mr. Mason's corporate attorney. Then Attorney Conner's spoke and said, "Has my client been charged? If not he has nothing further to say and he will be leaving with me, now. Let's go John."

John looked at Attorney Conner's and said, "Thanks." And he got up and walked towards the door.

Det. Riveria said, "I'll bet John here doesn't even know this legal eagle."

Then Det. Longstreet said, "Judging by the legal eagles shoes John couldn't even afford his retainer. I think this guy was hired by one of

John's silent partners. You know those guy's who like to take care of legal matters in house."

As John and Attorney Conner's stepped into the hallway they were pushed back into the room by Special Agent Ralph Bailey and Marshal's Harry Bailey and Laura McKnight.

Now the room is rather crowded and Det. Overstreet is confused about what is going on. Then Captain Frank Suozzi came into the room and said, "Gentlemen sorry I'm late but I just came down from the D.A.'s office with the news. This is Special Agent Ralph Bailey and his brother U.S. Marshal Harry Bailey and his associate Marshal Laura McKnight. And for our guest I am Det. Captain Frank Suozzi in charge of this squad. Now the long and short of this is you Mr. Mason are being handed over to the FBI on a murder and racketeering charge. One of the U.S. Attorney's will be down shortly to arraign you and your attorney can begin to earn his keep. Marshal's Bailey and McKnight on the other hand will be doing whatever they need to do within the confines of their joint investigation with the Fed's over here. And yes, the two Bailey's are brothers so whatever value that adds is whatever it adds. We'll if there are any further questions and you work for me, meet me in my office. On the other hand if you have any questions and you don't work for me, then I just can't help you. Ok? Ok! Let's clear this room we have a line waiting." And he walked out.

Then Agent Bailey said, "Counselor can we have a word with you and your client? And detectives may we have a moment with your former suspect?"

Both Det.'s Riveria and Overstreet got up and started to walk out, but they each turned one by one and looked at Agent Ralph and Marshal Harry and said, "Good thing you two weren't twins." They both laughed and walked out.

Attorney Conner's said, "Agent Bailey before you begin I'd like to have a word with my client. In private, please." Agent Bailey said, "Not until we charge and take full custody. Until then you can sit and listen or wait out side, it doesn't matter to me." Attorney Conner's responded and said, "How long have you been an Agent? Don't you know that this man still has rights?"

Agent Bailey looked at him and repeated this statement, you can wait in here or you can wait outside it doesn't matter to me. He doesn't have to answer any of my questions and if he wishes

The DEADLY MAILMAN

to leave and not wait for the formal charges he may go but I assure you there will be consequences, Mr. Mason. You see this guy, your attorney that is, was sent here by your partners Eddie and Joey Rocco. You know them, the guy's in the room with you when you shoot and killed Mr. Rosenberg. And by the way we also know you shot Joey in the shoulder, who quiet frankly did not really appreciate that, at all."

John sat with his mouth open for a moment and didn't say a word. Then there was a knock at the interrogation room door and in walked the U.S. Attorney.

Attorney Conner's quickly said, "Is there an offer?"

U.S. Attorney April Montgomery a tall full bodied young black woman said, "No, there is no offer we have video, audio and witnesses, your client is going away for a long time on this one. So you can sit back and collect your fee because he hasn't got a chance in hell of beating this."

Attorney Conner's smiled and said, "Well we'll see about that?" Then John said, "Surely there must be some kind of an offer on the table?" Attorney Conner's said, "Don't worry we got this." John looked at him and then at Marshal Bailey and Laura and said, "I need new counsel and then we can talk." Agent Bailey looked at Marshal Harry and said, "Would you hand this man a telephone?"

Rocco's Trucking and Moving Services

Eddie and Joey were drinking Sambocca at their desk when a call came in from Attorney Connor's. Patti handed Eddie the phone and Connor's explained that the fed's had taken Mason into custody and John was looking for his own attorney. He said, he believed that while there were no offers on the table and the fed's had him dead to rights on the murder of Attorney Rosenberg he feared that there was something else under the fed's sleeve.

Eddie thanked him and hung up. Then he turned to Joey and said, "I think its time that we sent our new parking lot king partner a message on how to keep his mouth shut?" Joey asked did we get that stock in the corporation yet? Eddie said, "Yes." Then Joey said, I agreed, let's send him a message." Then Eddie said, "Joey call Lou and tell him to do his mailman thing."

10:00 am at John Mason's Office the next

morning

Lou walks into John's office and when he saw John was in he walked over to the secretary's desk and asked her where he was. She said, "She hadn't seen him but he called and said he would be late. Then Lou asked her did John ever make a list of the properties he needed to complete the expansion and she gave him a copy. The next and final property on the list was that of a Harold Harper who lived in a small house right behind the barber shop Lou had acquired for John earlier.

Agent Ralph Bailey's Federal Plaza Office 10:00am that morning

Seated in the conference room of Agent Ralph Bailey's Federal Plaza office was Marshal Harry Bailey and Laura McKnight, John Mason and his attorney Zachary Weiss.

While Agent Ralph was explaining to Mason and his attorney the one and only offer the government was even willing to consider, should he successfully aid in their case against the Rocco crime family a urgent personal call came in for him.

When his secretary told him who it was he

decided to take the call in his office and leave the conference room for a few minutes.

On the phone was Phillip Westing Vice President for Nationwide Insurance Company. Mr. Westing explained the both the nature of Sam Gold's fraudulent insurance scheme, a prospective identity theft and a threat against his policy audit agent, Stanley Morrow and his family. Ralph tried to explain that he was in the middle of a high priority investigation and would not have time to look into the matter but Phillip reminded him of the confidence his firm had in him personally and asked him to reconsider. Ralph finally acquiesced and told him to forward their file over to his office and that he would get back to him later in the day.

Meanwhile back in the conference room Marshal Harry Bailey had received word that the surveillance team watching John Mason's office had spotted Lou Gallo and were in the process of following him.

On the way back to the conference room Ralph's secretary stopped him and handed him the preliminary file sent over by Phillip Westing concerning Sam Gold and the insurance fraud scam. Ralph took the file and carried it into the conference room and laid it on the table when he sat down.

Things began to move very fast at that point, Ralph began to prep John on the surveillance devised he was to keep with him when visiting the Rocco brothers and laid out the goals and objectives of what information he was to probe for. Particularly the whereabouts of Mr. Rosenberg's body and the decision to transport it to that particular parking lot and by who? Any information he could get concerning any other bodies would be helpful as well.

Once the meeting was over Mason was allowed to leave after he had made arrangements to meet and chat with the Rocco brothers later that evening.

As the group cleared the conference room Ralph got up and inadvertently left his Nationwide insurance fraud file behind but Marshal Laura grabbed it and she hurried to catch up with Harry and Ralph she dropped the file and the papers flew all over the hallway to Ralph's office. Both Ralph and Harry stopped and walked back to help her pick up the papers and Harry asked Ralph what that case was about. Ralph began to explain and just as Harry picked up the photo of Sam Gold and Ralph picked up the sketch of Lou Gallo the two men realized that they had both an insurance fraud, and identify theft case that tied into the Rocco family and John Mason racketeering case byway of Lou Gallo.

Marshal Bailey contacted the two detectives assigned to monitor John Mason's office looking for Lou Gallo. The men had Gallo under close watch and were following him uptown towards the Bronx River Parkway at that moment.

Harry instructed them that he was on his way to catch up with them and speak with Lou. They told him they could just stop him and hold him until he arrived but Harry was in downtown traffic and did not want to alarm Lou so he told them to stay close and keep in touch.

Lou took the Cross Bronx Expressway up into the Westchester Parkway towards Tuckahoe and almost lost the surveillance team but they maintained their cover. Finally Lou stopped in a parking lot and changed clothes into a mailman's uniform. The surveillance team just watched but kept Marshal Bailey updated as he speed towards the location.

The DEADLY MAILMAN

Once changed Lou left his car and pulled a mailbag out of his trunk and walked around the corner just out of sight of the detectives.

As Lou stood outside of Vince's apartment building he checked the mailboxes for names and apartment numbers. When he found the one he wanted he rang the bell and was buzzed in. Now all the detectives could do was sit in their car and wait for either Lou to return or Marshal Bailey to arrive.

Apartment 3G

Lou walked up the stairs to Apartment 3F and was directed to apartment 3G for Vince Carbone. Lou pulled his cap down kind of low to distort his eyes and knocked on Vince's door. Vince looked out and then realizing it was the mailman opened the door and stepped out. Lou handed him an express type envelope and asked him to sign his clipboard. When Vince signed the clipboard and took a closer look at the letter Lou gave him, Lou stabbed him in the neck and the stomach with an ice pick.

As Vince tried to grab for Lou, Lou stepped back into the stairwell and closed the door. Vince banged on the door several times but was loosing so much blood he quickly became dizzy fell down and bleeds out right there.

Lou wiped the blood off of his hand as he exited the stairwell in the lobby and slowly walked back around to his car and drove off.

Just then Marshal's Bailey and Laura caught up with the surveillance team and pushed to over take and stop Lou. But by then Lou had made it into traffic on the expressway and just pulled away from them. Harry called in an A.P.B. (All Point's Bulletin) on Lou's car when they lost him in traffic.

John Mason's Office

When John walked out of the Fed's office he immediately went to a bank to open a safe deposit box and then to his office to clean out the wall safe. As soon as he stepped off of the elevator his secretary told him that the Rocco brothers had called five times, but he interrupted her and said, "Get Vince Carbone on the phone I need to talk to him immediately" and just as he opened his office door, she said and, he saw three of Eddie Rocco's men sitting at his desk.

John calmly walked in and one man said, "Mr. Rocco wants to see you, now!" John smiled as he looked up at the 6'6" 350 lb muscle bound brut and said, "Which one?" The man grabbed John around the neck and lifted him up into the air and said, "Does it really matter? Really? Let's go." And he dropped him on the floor. John straightened himself up and turned to leave and one of the other men said, "The Boss said don't forget the money." The first brut grabbed John from behind and said, "Wait a minute, open the safe. The boss wants you to bring all of the money, too." John turned and looked at the safe and then at the brut and said, "I don't have the combination."

That was when the brut got angry and slammed John into the office door, head first, breaking his nose. Then he picked him up and carried him back into the office and body slammed him on the desk. John bounced so high his arms touched the chandelier. Then the three men grabbed John, one his head and shoulders, the other his feet and the last his torso and they went to through him through the office window, again and John screamed out, "Ok, Ok! I remember it."

That was when they put him down in front of the safe and handed him two suitcases. While John was loading the cash into the suitcases his secretary came in and said, "Mr. Mason the police were answering Vince's cellphone should I speak to them?" John looked at her and she realized that he didn't want to be disturbed so she backed back out of the office and said, "I'll tell them it wasn't important" and she closed the door.

Old Man Harper's Place

Old man Harper better known as Harold H. Harper was a long time resident of the Flatbush community. He was a widower with no heirs and a cat lover. Harold Harper was an 80 year old World War II Veteran and retired railroad worker. His favorite past time was sitting on his front porch and watching the gang members come and go with their loot and drug money from the house across the street from him.

John Mason had approached Mr. Harper several times over the last six months in hopes of buying his parcel to complete his parking garage idea. Harper's location would have made the difference between 100 car multi-tier lot and a 200 car multi-tier lot.

John had offered Old Man Harper $1 million dollars for his 150' x 300' lot, eventhough it was worth $2 million, and Harper knew what it was worth.

Lou's plan was simple get Harper to sign a quick claim deed and take the money or kill him and forge the claim deed and take $250 large from Mason.

Still wearing his postal workers uniform Lou made his way from Tuckahoe to Flatbush with an eye to kill Old Man Harper and make this last big money score off of Mason.

When Lou arrived at the Harper's house he parked around the corner at the Laundromat got his mailbag out of the back seat and slowly walked around to Harpers place. When he got there he walked right up the front steps to the porch where Old Man Harper was sitting in his rocking chair and reading the paper when Lou stepped on the porch. Lou said, "You Harold Harper? I got a special delivery for you." Old Man Harper put the newspaper down in his lap and said, "Well this must be special usual Ronnie Lutz my regular mailman delivers those special packages to me. What is it this time? Playboy? Gentlemen's Quarters? Or "Dirty Old Men?" They both laughed.

But as Harper laughed Lou pulled out an express envelope with one hand and his ice pick with the other and leaned into old man Harper and stuck him under his rib cage right into the heart. The blood came gushing down his shirt and into the waistband of his pants as he fell back into his rocking chair.

Lou looked to see if there was anyone on the street and seeing no one he pushed Old Man Harpers rocking chair back into the front door, through the livingroom and into the kitchen to the breakfast table.

He looked around and through the kitchen drawers until he saw something with Harpers signature on it. Then he sat down and forged Harpers name on the quick claim deed notarized it and left with it through the rear door.

CHAPTER 9

CLEANING HOUSE

Starlet Ballroom in Bensonhurst Queens Mark Oliver's Retirement Party

Seated at the bar of the Starlet Ballroom in Bensonhurst were John Mason and several other City Councilmen drinking and celebrating Councilmen Mark Oliver's retirement. No one wants to dim the hour with conversation as to why Oliver was forced into retirement but with the special election to seat a replacement for him scheduled for the next day everyone tried hard to stay in a good mood.

When Mark finally made his way over to the bar John greeted him with a warm huge and a kiss on the cheek, which caused a stir of laughter.

After john ordered his final round of drinks in Marks honor, he and john stepped to the end of the bar to privately chat for a few minutes. John overviewed the difficulties he was facing since Fred had died and he thanked mark for all that he did for him while he was in office.

Mark subtly reminded John that he was merely

retiring not dying and that he would be available for private consultations as need be for his usual fee for services. John laughed and said, "If you only had as much expertise in criminal law as you have in City politics and real estate law things might be very different right about now." Mark looked at him, and said, "Remember any problem can be resolved for the right amount of money. The trick is never run short on money when you have big problems." Both men laughed and John said, "By the way have you ever encountered people like Eddie Rocco or his little brother Joey Rocco?"

Mark put his drink down and said, "So those are your new partners? The people the Fed's have put you at odds with? God help you John. Those are bad people. They'd just as soon shot you and your whole family as to look at you when it comes to money. Don't get me wrong they have a lot of money but they just aren't the type to be reasonable for any length of time, so be very careful. Ok?"

John chugged down his drink and placed the glass on the bar and said, "Too late." And then he started to walk away. Mark reached for him and said, "If you really get in a pinch call me, I still have a few friends in high places." John turned and said, "If they are not sitting on the top floor of 26 Federal Plaza they aren't gonna be much help to me right now." Mark said, "Don't under estimate the power of a retiring politician my friend." John nodded and walked away.

As John walked through the catering hall lobby he sensed he was being followed but he couldn't put his finger on any one individual who might be following him. He figured it was the Fed's since they were eagerly awaiting his meeting with the Rocco brothers but John knew he needed a few minutes alone to contact Vince and give him some final instruction about Lou. John wanted Lou dead before the Fed's could track him down and turn him against him.

Finally on his way to the front valet parking area john slipped into a men's room and borrowed the attendant's cellphone and attempted to call Vince; but when the phone rang a strange voice answered and john just hung up. He remembered what his secretary said earlier so he figured Vince was either in detention or interrogation and he just went on to get his car and go meet with the Rocco Brothers.

Midnight at Pier 12 Rocco Brothers N. J.

Trucking and Moving Warehouse

John pulled into a loading bay and parked. He could see Eddie and Joey standing on the loading dock but he knew if he got out to approach them he would be searched and if they found the bug the Fed's placed in his jacket button this would be their last meeting and it wouldn't end pleasantly for him. So he patiently waited until they summoned him over.

When they finally did he just left his jacket in the car but he left the windows down just in case he could get them to walk over to the car.

When John walked up on the loading dock two of Eddie's men searched him while Joey just looked at him hoping they'd find something but they didn't. So the three men stood on the loading dock for a minute until a couple of Eddie's men brought out some folding chairs and a bottle of wine.

John talked about the interrogation at great length until both Eddie and Joey screamed enough.

Finally Eddie said, "I'm not to happy with the way you have disrespected me and Joey over there. I sent a car for you and the car comes back but you're not in it. What's up with that?" John said, "Well I appreciate the escort but my mentor and benefactor was having his retirement party and I had to make an entrance. Nothing personal, just business, you know?"

Eddie nodded and said, "I could understand that, it would have been nice if you'd called but that's neither here nor there. Let's talk about the money. We lent you $3 million you returned $1.25 million, explain that."

John told Eddie he completed two of the last three transactions and the third transaction cost him much less then he had planned on, so he had the $1.25 mil left over. John said, "He was going to stop by on Monday when the dust settled from the last transaction and clear things up with the money but all of those other things broke out, the whole Rosenberg body in his car trunk, the self serving corporate lawyer and the Fed's issue as I explained earlier.

Eddie said, "yea, yea, yea...about that Rosenberg thing, let's not gloss over that. That was pretty funny huh? Him being dead, because you killed him in a fit of whatever, you walking out and leaving him in my cousin's den and him turning up your trunk in front of the police. Pretty funny huh? A classic."

Eddie continued and said, "You know you are a pretty lucky guy? Most people don't get to make more than one mistake before they wind up dead of un-natural causes around here." Joey grunts and then smiles. Then Eddie said, "So what happened with our legal eagle? You know he still charged us for the consultation even though you didn't partake of his services. He's a pretty good attorney you know. Cost me $2,500 an hour or part there of."

John smiled and said, "I really didn't think he had my best interest at heart."

Eddie said, "Well the one thing he did have at heart was our interest. Now how do you suppose to repay the $1.75 million you owe us on the loan, it's interest which is set just a little over prime at, let's say 24% per day ad then buy out our 50% interest in the business? Which is probably worth...oh! I say! Another $5 to $10 mil?"

John smiled and said, "I got no intentions of repaying the loan or buying you out."

Eddie looked at Joey and Joey said, "That's a

pretty good attitude for a dead man."

Eddie shock his head yes and then said to John, "Oh! Really?"

John smiled again and said, "I'm going to let you two buy me out. You can make me an offer for my shares of the stock, and forgive the loan in exchange for me keeping quiet about all of those people you've murdered amassing the parking lot empire you now control."

Eddie looked at Joey and Joey looked at John and then back at Eddie and all three men broke out laughing for almost a whole minute.

Finally Eddie stops laughing and Joey pulls out his s&w .38 and places it at John temple and john stops laughing. But before Joey can pull the trigger Eddie said, "Hold it Joey. This guy is a piece of work and he's funny too. But he is smart." Then Eddie turned to john and said, "And so what do you have up your sleeve that is going to keep me from letting Joey do you right here? Because you can blame six, seven hell even sixty seven bodies on us, not one is going to stick. So what you got? That's gonna keep you alive until the morning?"

John looked Eddie square in the eyes and said,

The DEADLY MAILMAN

"Lou Gallo has made over $30 million dollars in the last five years. Did you know that?"

Both Eddie and Joey's jaws dropped right to the floor. Neither one said a word, and then John said, "I guess not? So how could Lou Gallo make so much money and still be available to do odd jobs for you and not share a nickel of his gold mine with either of you, his mentors. And I use that word loosely."

Angry now Eddie told Joey to send a crew over to Lou's place and bring him here. Joey said, "Why don't we just call him, he'll come over. He doesn't know that we know what he has been doing." Eddies responded and said, "I want him here right now. Do you hear me?"

Then John said, "I don't know about you but if my homicidal manic of a boss called me or sent a crew to pick me up at this time of night I'd be ready to do battle. If there is one thing about Lou he is a creature of habit. Now tomorrow morning I expect to see for a couple of reasons. One he is due to check the books and two he is due to pick up this weeks vig; which by the way you have already collected right there in the bag. So why don't you just send a crew over in the morning and meet him in my office around 10:00am?"

Eddie smiled and shock his head and Joey agreed.

Surveillance Van parked six blocks away

Both Special Agent Ralph Bailey and U.S. Marshal Harry Bailey high five themselves for planting that extra bug in John's shoe, so when John began to lay out Lou Gallo's identity theft and insurance fraud scheme and how he had killed so many people in the furtherance of a mob takeover of a small business it was like a road map for convicting all four men.

John's version of things put everything together so neatly it was a nice, 'you conned me but I conned you conspiracy'.

The next morning at John Mason's Office 10:00am

Waiting inside Mason's office is Eddie Rocco's crew of three men. One seated just inside the office door on its right side and the other two seated on the left side. John was seated behind his desk right in front of the door and in front of the wall of plate glass windows those same guy's through him out of a couple of weeks earlier.

The DEADLY MAILMAN

John's secretary Sara Banks was seated at the reception desk in the lobby as usual.

Outside in the front and rear 100 car parking lot were three unmarked sedans and one unmarked surveillance van parked on a side street. Along with the three unmarked cars there were four plain clothes detectives waiting in the lobby area; one by the front entrance, one by the rear entrance, one by the elevator banks and one roaming around the newspaper stand.

Marshal's Bailey and Laura were in the surveillance van around the corner.

At 9:45am Lou Gallo pulled up about three car lengths from the rear parking lot entrance and parked. He sat there for a moment and then he got out of the car and slowly walked along the fence line towards the rear entrance of the building. As he got close to the double doors, but still standing along the fence line he noticed a linen truck parked along the fence line with all of its doors open. The truck was none descript but there were two men working in it. One had just loaded a bungle of white uniforms and towels into a rolling cart and was pushing it towards the rear entrance doors. As he approached a man dressed in street clothes walked over and looked into the cart then he waved the delivery man in. Lou immediately knew that something was wrong. So when the second man loaded up his cart and walked towards the rear doors the same plain clothes detective checked his cart and then waved him inside, just as the first man was walking out this time without a cart.

Lou stepped into the truck and waited out of sight until the deliveryman climbed inside. Then Lou handed him a $100 bill and pointed to the empty last remaining empty cart that he wanted to get inside and go in the building. The deliveryman, an Hispanic teenager shrugged his shoulders and said, "Si". Lou climbed in and sat low in the cart holding his s&w .38 under his jacket so the boy could see.

The boy covered just enough of Lou up so he could see out but not be seen and he began to roll the cart out towards the building rear entranceway.

When he approached the doorway the detective looked at him and the boy nodded and then he waved the boy inside. Once inside the boy pushed the cart over to the service elevator and rang for it. Lou looked up and the boy signaled no not yet and Lou sat back down. When the elevator door opened the boy pushed the cart inside and said, "Senor I send the elevator down to the basement and leave do you want to go to the basement?" Lou said, "No" and he showed the boy four fingers. The boy said I press the fourth floor for you. If you come back this way soon I take you back out to the truck and maybe you give me a few more dollars?" Lou shook his head yes and said, "Si."

Once upstairs Lou stepped off of the service elevator and looked directly at Sara Banks. As he approached her he could see she was nervous, so he pulled out his s&w .38 and put on its silencer and instead of bypassing her and walking into John's office he walked right up on her and said, "I need you to open the office door." She timidly shook her head no and said, "It is alright you can walk right in."

Lou stepped around the reception desk and grabbed her arm, pulling her out of her seat and said, "Right in to a death trap, right?"

Lou pulled and shoved her to the door and when they were there and she was standing in between him and the door he reached around her and opened the door then pushed her inside.

The DEADLY MAILMAN

The door opened wide from the force and swung full open to the right. Lou pushed Sara so hard she stumbled in to the left of the door and bumped into the gun man seated there. Lou stepped inside and shot twice to the left killing the gun man Sara had fallen into. Then he quickly fired three shots to through the door on his right, and he could hear the two men fall to the floor.

John grabbed for his desk drawer and Lou draw down on him and said, "That's not a smart move, my friend" and John put his hands up and froze.

Just then Sara realized that the gun man Lou had just killed was bleeding on her and she started to hyperventilate. Lou closed the office door behind him and as he survived the two men behind it he said to the Sara, "Shut up before I silence you like I did them." Sara immediately pulled herself together and shut up.

Lou looked at John and then walked over to him and shoved him and his chair against the window bank. Then he opened John's desk drawer and took out his handgun, a glock 9. He checked the load and saw that it had 15 shots in it then he cocked it and pointed it at John and put his s&w in his waistband. Lou grabbed the curtain strings and pulled them closed.

He told John to get up and sit on the floor and he took and sat in john's chair behind the desk. Sara was quaking in her heels so hard that Lou said, "You over there knock it off before I knock you off. You're a distraction."

Lou looked at John and said, "So you tried my own people against me? For what? Oh! Let me guess you had no choice but to save your own skin. I can imagine that."

John said, "There is a lot of heat on out there and you my friend are the one with the most flexibility."

Lou said, "Flexibility! I never had the balls to put it that way but we'll see how this works out. So where is the money?"

John said, "What money, your bosses took it all back yesterday. It's gone."

Lou said, "Oh! No. I'm talking about your money. Where is it?"

John said, "What are you deaf? I said, Eddie's boys took it all yesterday. It's gone."

Sara said, "I know where it is." John said, "Bitch

keep your mouth shut before I shut it for you."

Lou looked at John and then at his gun and said, "No, you shut up before I shut you up, permanently. Ok! Lady you got the floor, talk fast."

Sara said, "So what's in it for me if I tell you?"

John said, "Shut up Sara. I'm not going to tell you again."

Lou walked over to john and hit him in the head with the butt of the gun. He hit him so hard it draw blood. Then he said, "Open you mouth again and I'll put another hole in your head. Now lay on the floor stomach first."

Then Lou said, "You lady, stand up." Sara pushed the dead bloody man off of her, stood up, straightened her skirt and said, "All I want is what is mine and I'm out of here." Lou said, "Why you married?" Sara said, "Engaged." Lou said, "Got children?" Sara said, "A 6 year old." Lou said, "Got a drivers license?" Sara reached in the back pocket of her jeans and pulled out her wallet and handed Lou her license.

Lou looked at it and said, "This were you live now?" Sara said, yes.

The DEADLY MAILMAN

Lou said, "Ok! Ms. Sara Banks with a 6 year old who is engaged and lives at 450 River Drive, Bronxville, tell me what you know."

Sara said, "There is a floor safe. Over there under the chair you usually sit in."

Lou walked around the desk and pushed the chair away and pulled back the area rug and saw the trap door. Then he opened it and saw the floor safe. It required a combination for the lock. Lou looked at John and said, "What's the combo?" John said, "Kill me. I'll never tell you. That is all the money I got in the world. Sara how could you do this?"

Lou looked at Sara and said, "Do you know the combination?" Sara said, "No. Why? It's always unlocked."

Lou looked at John with a twinkle I his eye and said, "Oh! Really." Then he reached down and tried the lock and it opened.

Lou looked inside and said to Sara, go get me a shipping box, some clear tape and a UPS, Fedex air bill. Hurry up will ya?" Then Lou started pulling stacks of cash out of the safe.

When Sara came back Lou grabbed the box

and said to John, "What you got in here half a mil?"

Lou started to stack the money into the shipping box. Then he pulled out three packs of $20 or $15,000 and handed it to Sara. Sara smiled and said, "How about a couple more? You know for retirement." Lou looked at her and then she said, "A girl had to ask."

Lou finished taping up the box and prepared the shipping receipt and told Sara, "You go into the bathroom over there, when the police come you come out. You better find a nice hiding place for your cash they are probably going to search you before they let you go."

When Sara went into John's private bathroom and closed the door. John said, "So I guess this is it?"

Lou reached in his jacket pocket and pulled out a one way microphone and placed it under John's desk chair. Then he walked over to John and said, "You know, you were right; this is it" and he shot him in the back of the head.

Lou grabbed the box of cash and took the elevator downstairs to the basement to the building mailroom and placed it in the outgoing mail box. Then when he took the elevator up to the first floor he pulled the fire alarm and complete chaos over took the building. As people started to run out into the parking lot he just joined in and walked right by the detective monitoring the rear lobby exit door.

10:30am John Mason's Office

By the time Marshal Bailey and Laura got to John's office the Fire Marshal's had just gone through and found the four bodies and Sara Banks sitting in the private bathroom.

A couple of the surveillance team detectives had taken Sara to another office to wait for Harry and Laura while the Coroner and the forensic teams were going over the crime scene.

Harry could see that Sara was visibly shaken so he asked Marshal Laura to lead the interview.

Sara was open and forthcoming, not knowing much about the business dealing of john mason and the people he associated with. Things seemed to go rather routinely until Marshal Laura asked Sara why she thought Lou Gallo would leave her unharmed. Sara changed her story several times before Marshal Bailey stepped I and said, "Did he threaten you?" Sara nodded and broke down crying saying yes, yes he threatened my son's life and he told me if I said anything he would track me down and kill me.

Then Harry said, "So what did you do for him?"

Sara pulled herself together and stopped crying and said, "I didn't do anything, all I did was what he asked me, nothing else."

Harry looked at her and one of the forensic team members walked in and pulled harry to the side for a moment and when he returned he smiled and said, "So how much did he pay you for telling him about the floor safe?"

Sara's mouth dropped to the floor and she said, "He didn't pay me anything. What floor safe?"

Harry said, "Now look this is how this works. This is a homicide investigation. During same if we come across another crime we are not compelled to disclose it unless we believe it is material to concluding our investigation. Now is the time to come clean. If I have to dig into your statement and find problems then you will be found to be hindering my investigation and subject to the full extent of the law, including any illegal activities directly resulting from said hindrance or indirectly hindering same. Is that clear? Now let's have it."

Sara began to well up and explain exactly what had happened, even the money she got from Lou for pointing out the floor safe.

Marshal Bailey told her she would not be charged but cash she received would have to be confiscated as evidence of Lou Gallo's alleged robbery of the victim. But she would be able to get it back after the trial. With that Sara was very relieved and was allowed to leave.

Then Marshal Bailey and Laura went into the crime scene office and as they looked over it another forensic investigator came into the room and said, "Marshal's we have the office security video cued up would you like to view it now?"

When they got down to the basement mailroom Marshal Bailey noticed the clerks wrapping up the days work and loading up separate binds for the outside couriers to pick up.

After viewing the office security tape Marshal Bailey hurried out of the security office to the parcel staging area outside the mailroom and saw that it was empty; so he had one of the remaining crime scene officer's go and track down the FedEx pick up driver for Lou's package.

8:00pm 26 federal Plaza 13th Floor FBI Regional offices

Both Marshal's Bailey and Laura where just as confused as Bailey's brother Ralph was when the forensic teams lead investigator reported to them that a audio devise was found under a chair in John Mason's office.

When the group looked back over the security footage they could see that Lou planted it but could not understand why until Harry figured it out.

Marshal Bailey concluded that the reason Lou wanted to keep an eye on what happened at the crime scene was for two reasons. First he needed to see if our witness the receptionist talked and secondly, but more importantly he wanted to know if we found out about the money parcel.

When Harry revealed those possible motives everyone pondered how smart this guy Gallo really was. Then the officer Harry had sent to retrieve the FedEx package Lou had mailed out arrived with the parcel. Harry took charge of it and examined the delivery instructions and then asked Ralph if he'd call the station Manager and find out how they could keep the tracking information real time while they figured out the best way to control how the package got to the suspect.

After some time it was decided that a dummy package would be substituted and go through the delivery system and the Marshal's would track it and then switch the actual delivery driver with Harry at the arrival place and time. The delivery address was 2130 Apartment 3, Pacific View Parkway, Encino, California. Marshal Laura google mapped the address and found that it was a mailbox operation, and the delivery date was the next morning at 8:00am.

Marshal Bailey immediately call the Marshal's office in Encino California and requested a team be sent to that address that night, find the owner or whoever was scheduled to open the office in the morning and keep them from opening it until he and Marshal Laura got there. Then Agent Ralph called and checked on all flights leaving the tri-state area that with or without connection could get someone there before 8:00am the next morning. While Ralph was waiting for an answer his secretary came into the conference room and told him he had an important call on his private line, so he left the conference room to take it.

When he returned Marshal Bailey and Laura were about to get up and leave to catch an official jet to Encino. Ralph asked where they were going and when Harry explained Ralph said, you might want to hold off on that flight until you hear what I just learned. Harry and Laura sat back down and waited for Ralph to explain.

CHAPTER 10

HABEUS CORPUS

Agent Ralph Bailey spoke and said, "An old friend of mine a top executive in the insurance industry just called to tell me that Sam Gold aka Lou Gallo or someone associated with his insurance agency filed a death benefit claim against a $1,000,000 whole life policy in the name of John Mason and wanted to stop by and pick up the benefits check in the morning if possible."

Harry looked at Laura and they both busted out laughing. Then Ralph looked around and started to laugh as well.

Then finally Ralph asked Harry what he thought would be the best course of action. Harry thought for a moment and said, "Well we know he is going to go to Encino to pick up that cash. I think whenever he does it really won't matter if we tell the proprietor to hold the box or not, Lou will just kill him and take it because he would absolutely nothing to lose then. But picking up the death benefits check is just a rouse. He knows he won't be able to cash that or even deposit it without giving his location away. My money is on the Encino pick up. If anything he can always call on the benefits check and have them mail it if they decide to even give it to him."

Ralph smiled and said, "I guess I'll see you two when you get back from Encino?"

6:00am Mailboxes –R—Us, 2130 Pacific View Parkway, Encino, CA

Parked outside and about a half a block down the street in a black on black 2010 Ford Tarsus 4 door sedan was Marshal's Harry Bailey and Laura McKnight. Parked a half a block up from them on the other side of the street was Marshal Alex Lipton with his partner Doug Thomas both of the Encino CA Regional Office. There were two cars parked in the rear of the building following the same surveillance strategy.

Encino is a heavily populated residential community resting on the Pacific Ocean coast line and as usual the day's weather was shaping up as to be expected, hot and sunny with a cold breeze off the ocean. Sunrise was 5:45am and the streets were packed with foot traffic, and plenty of parked cars from the beach going traffic.

Marshal Bailey, as did all of the members of his

Fugitive Takedown Team, had a photo of Lou Gallo taped to his dashboard and discreetly used a set of binoculars to canvas the crowd of people on the street while looking for Lou Gallo to approach the Mailbox store.

It seemed like an impossible task as the day wore on and the crowd at the beach grow and grow.

The FedEx delivery truck showed up at its regular time, 8:30am and dropped the dummy box along with several other parcels and express envelopes but when the Store Manager stepped out side to greet him Harry noticed something strange about him. Eventhough he was parked almost half a block away and trying see through the crowd of people he felt that either the driver or the Store Manager didn't really know or recognize the other.

When Harry mentioned this oddity to Marshal Laura she question what if anything he really see through the crush of people.

That was when Harry jumped out of the car and walked up to the store.

As Harry walked up to the store and watched the FedEx delivery driver unloaded the boxes from the rear of his truck onto his hand truck harry noticed that driver kept looking into the back of the truck as if he was getting direction from someone inside.

When Harry got close enough he could hear someone inside the truck pulling boxes and sitting them down hard on the tail of the truck.

Strategically standing to the far side of the truck so the Store Manager couldn't see Harry looking into the FedEx truck Harry looked inside and saw a in a FedEx uniform handing packages out of the back of the truck to the driver. Harry listened for a minute and he heard the two men talking.

One man said to the other, 'I never saw this guy before in my life and I've been dropping this route for over five years now. It's always the owner who opens up and signs for the deliveries. This guy doesn't even know where the signature line is on the airbills...' Harry stepped back and texted Marshal Laura asking her to check with the mailbox store owner by phone to see if it is really him in the store right now.

Marshal Laura called the store and a man answered the phone, when she asked who it was he said, his name was Lou and the owner was out sick. Then he said, he would have the manager call her back later in the afternoon and hung up before he could get her phone number. Marshal Laura texted Harry that she thought something might be wrong. Harry told Laura to contact the other Marshal's and have them converge on the Store but not to enter until he gave the signal.

Within a minute there were four armed Marshal's at the rear door along with Harry and Laura and two other officers at the front door.

When Harry saw that the last box, the dummy box was being loaded on the drivers hand truck he decided that it was time to make the move. He and Marshal Alex walked in the front the door in front of the driver with the hand truck and Marshal Laura and Alex's partner followed the driver with the hand truck in. Simultaneously the other Marshal's stepped in store through the rear door, where they found the Store Owner tied and gagged in the rest room.

But as the rear door opened a small door bell went off alerting the Lou that while someone was coming in the front door which he could see there was some one else coming in the back door which he couldn't see.

Lou took cover and fired four shots at Marshal Bailey and the team coming in the front door, hitting Marshal Alex in the leg, and the delivery driver in the head, killing him instantly.

Both Harry and Laura and the third officer took cover and but didn't fire back. Marshal Alex's partner helped him back out of the front door and called for back up. White the officers in the rear of the store took cover while one of them drug the owner out of the rest room through the rear door and into the parking lot to safety.

Then Harry shouted to Lou, "You're surrounded Lou, give it up. You don't stand a chance and with this dead courier over here and you being in the state of California if we don't take you in and the local's show up it's going to be the chair. So what do you say Lou? We don't have much time, here."

It was quiet for a minute and then Lou said, "I got one of you and a passerby, why don't you guy's give up and I'll let you live."

Marshal Bailey just shook his head and didn't say a word.

The DEADLY MAILMAN

Lou repeated his statement and then there was a single shot fired and all you could hear was a gun fall to the floor. Then it was so quiet you could hear the sweat on the Marshal's foreheads rolling down their faces.

So Harry spoke and said, "Lou you alright? ...Lou! You still there?"

Then it became clear, Lou had been hit and had fallen behind the counter. Harry cautiously made his way around the left side of the room while the Marshal's in the rear slipped into the main room to the right side.

When Harry reached Lou, Lou was out cold and bleeding heavily from the top of his forehead. It looked as if Harry's bullet had just creased Lou's head.

Back in the Prison Recreation Yard

...Lou smiled at Roscoe and said, "I thought I was a goner but if it wasn't for that old postal carrier cap I was wearing I might not be here telling you this story." Roscoe shook his head and said, "So man, tell me they didn't find your stash." Lou stopped smiling and said, "Why! You thinking of becoming my special friend so you can

Con me out of it?"

Roscoe waved his hands and said, "No, no man. I was just asking that's all!"

Then Lou looked around a couple of times and leaned into Roscoe as if he wanted to whisper something in his ear. When Roscoe came close Lou said, "They'll never find it. They'll never find my stash because I spent it on my way to from the airport. So don't bother trying to guess. And when I get out of here I'm gonna be on easy street. So stick around maybe I can use a guy like you when I get out. I'll teach you the business. There has never been a Black Mofia? Maybe I'll tell you how to start one."

The End

The DEADLY MAILMAN

LIST OF OTHER TITLES BY THIS AUTHOR
INCLUDING
U.S. Marshal Harry Bailey, and the
"The Parables of Life Series"

Title	RELEASE DATES
1- U.S. Marshal Harry Bailey and the case Of the Persistent Widow	February 2013
2- U.S. Marshal Harry Bailey and the case Of the Wicked Farmers	May 2013
3- U.S. Marshal Harry Bailey and the case Of the Minas	September 2013
4- U.S. Marshal Harry Bailey and the case Of the Hidden Treasure	December 2013
5- U.S. Marshal Harry Bailey and the case Of the Friend at Midnight	March 2014
6- U.S. Marshal Harry Bailey and the case Of the Foolish Virgins	June 2014
7- U.S. Marshal Harry Bailey and the case Of the Good Samaritan	December 2014
8- U.S. Marshal Harry Bailey and the case Of the Four Soils	May 2015
9- U.S. Marshal Harry Bailey and the case Of the Lost Coin	September 2015
10-U.S. Marshal Harry Bailey and the case Of the Prodigal Son	December 2015
11- U.S. Marshal Harry Bailey and the case Of the Two Debtors	March 2016
12- U.S. Marshal Harry Bailey and the case Of the Two Sons	September 2016

Ask about our SPECIAL EDITION of U.S. Marshal Harry Bailey and the case of the CORPORATE KILLINGS available now!
www.usmarshalharrybailey.com
Other titles: The Way Station, U.S. Marshal Harry Bailey and the Corporate Killings and The Game of Your Life, 2-1-1 Emergency, Clinical Trials, Criminal Mastermind, To Hell for the Holidays and look out for the 6 volume series U.S. Marshal Harry Bailey and the "City of Prophesy" series coming in 2015.

www.ingramcontent.com/pod-product-compliance
Lightning Source LLC
Chambersburg PA
CBHW070614130626
46556CB00001B/368